RIDE
Hard

HEATHER LEIGH

To my husband,

without your support I wouldn't
have had the "balls" to do this.

To my angel here on earth, Sofia,

Mama loves you.

To my family, friends and co-workers,

for their love and support.

To the many amazing people,

for their support and help along my journey to becoming an Indie Author.

To the readers, bloggers, and promoters

who have read Burning Desire, and wanted more,
I am so touched and flattered; I hope you love Ride Hard.

To all the smut book lovers and MC junkies,

here's another one to add to the collection.

BURNING DESIRE

Condemned Angels MC Series, #1

Jeremy Moretti and Chase DeLuca have grown up together and into different MCs. Their lives were promised and destined to the Condemned Angels and Hell's Rebels. As they grew, so did Chase's feelings for Jeremy's younger sister, Roxanne.

Stemming from separate clubs, they have all the stakes against them. Michael Moretti, President of the Condemned Angels has forewarned Chase to stay away from his daughter. There is too much at risk and clubs stick to their own kind. No mixing whatsoever.

The years apart have done them good, however, Roxanne has finished school and is back home, and back in Chase's life. However, she isn't alone. Roxanne is dating the Treasurer of her father's club.

Things start to go wrong, as their secret feelings grow stronger for one another. Will Chase fight for what has always been his, or will the MC stand in his way?

Get your copy of Burning Desire NOW

PRAISE FOR BURNING DESIRE

"The sexual tension was through the roof, and not only between the main characters. They get so close and then something stops them. This happened so many times, by the time they actually did come together the sex was exploding out of my e-reader."
- **Lost In A Book**

"Burning Desire is the first book in the Condemned Angels MC series, and boy let me tell you – it is a raw, dirty, dangerous MC story. As a new author, Heather certainly has brought her A game, and she most definitely turned up the heat with the deliciously sexy male lead – Chase."
- **Deliciously Wicked Books**

"Heather Leigh's writing is new to me, and I'm so glad I had the chance to pick this one up. Her writing is realistic and fast paced with plenty of action. Her steamy scenes are fantastic, and her characters have depth that keeps the scenes going."
- **Two Moms Reading**

"I loved Roxy's smart mouth, spit fire attitude from the beginning and Chase, omg Chase!! He was seriously one of the sexiest male lead characters I have read in a while!"
- **Summer's Book Blog**

"There were plenty of surprises and I was left wanting more. If you are looking for a new MC series to fall in love with this is the one for you. I loved the characters, story, and pretty much everything else about the book. I'm looking forward to reading more in this series."
- **Love Between the Sheets**

"This book was wonderful from beginning to end. I loved every minute of it. It as like Romeo and Juliette with hotter men, sexier scenes and MC's."
- **Jodie's Wine List**

"Just WOW, like really WOW this story I was able to start and finish it in one day it blew my freaking mind away."
- **Whispered Thoughts**

PROLOGUE
Four Months Later

CHASE

"HEY BIG BOY, LOOKS LIKE YOU NEED SOME COMPANY." I FELT A PAIR OF LIPS GRAZE my earlobe as I tossed back the shot of whiskey and curled my lips over my teeth. I slammed the shot glass down on the bar, and looked over to whoever was talking to me. Some new girl, looking for a good fuck, and she was looking in the wrong fucking place for it. The music pounded its way through the clubhouse. We had a full house for the celebration of uniting the Condemned Angels and the Hell's Knights. Our patch over was in full effect. The place was packed tonight, brothers from all over were helping us party hard tonight.

I felt her small hands smooth over my shoulder and down my back. My eyes closed, seeing Roxy's face. I quickly shook my head of the memory of her. Four fucking months! Four months since I've seen or heard from her. She's probably due any day now, if she hasn't already had the baby. My chest ached, thinking about my child being born into this world without me there fucking killed me. I can only hope that I'll be a part of its life.

"I'm not for you, sweetheart." I looked up at her. She was a petite thing; bleach blond hair and big tits. I wasn't even fucking interested. Apparently my dick was broken when it came to chicks. There was only one out there, and she fucking wants nothing to do with me. Moretti won't even tell me where she is. Only that she is safe, in good hands and not to track her down. She couldn't live with the possibility that her baby is Jake's. She didn't want to bring bad blood to her club, or some crazy shit like that.

"You sure, baby?" she filled my shot glass for me, giving me those fuck me eyes.

"He's good, Gina. Let him be," I heard Hunter's voice call over. Shit, he was always looking out for me since she upped and disappeared.

"Brother." I saluted him before I put the shot glass to my lips and tipped my head back.

"Think you've had enough. Fucking drowning your sorrows in here isn't going to help you get her back." He started to clean up around me.

"Ha! Get her back? She fucking left me, Hunter. Too scared to take a chance. She's keeping me away from my own fucking baby. I fucking miss her." I threw the glass and it shattered against the floor.

"I know, Brother, you can't fucking give up like this. Maybe she will come back." He patted my shoulder.

"You know something I don't?" I look up at him, seeing double.

"Um..." he hesitated. I jumped off the bar stool and grabbed him by the collar of his shirt.

"What the fuck do you know?" I pinned my best friend to the wall.

"Chill the fuck out, Chase. This is exactly why I didn't want to say anything in the first place. You have to get control of your shit. You have been drinking yourself under the table almost every night." He pushed me off of him.

I grabbed my beer off the bar, and took a swig. Hunter ripped the bottle from my lips.

"What the fuck? If you're not going to tell me shit, then what else can I do?" I yelled at him.

"Fucking listen to me, you dick," he yelled back. We were the only two at the back bar. I took a seat back on my stool.

"I overheard, Moretti...she's coming back home."

"When?" I went to stand up but Hunter put a hand to my chest,

2

forcing me back down.

"She's already been back."

"What?" I was fucking pissed. I balled my fists on the tops of my knees.

"Just the other night. It's on the DL. She hasn't figured shit out yet, didn't want anyone to know she was back. Stayed with one of Charlie's nieces, a couple towns over. I don't know. I'm not even supposed to know this shit." He rubbed the back of his neck, looking up at me while trying to gauge my reaction.

"A couple fucking towns over? How the fuck could no one find her?"

"Moretti's orders, to not find her."

"Fuck. If she thought that baby is mine, which it is; then she should have fucking stayed." I shook my head back and forth.

"Maybe she will come around, Chase. You got to see shit from her point of view."

"You think I fucking haven't? I thought about that shit twenty-four seven since she has been gone. Everything I come up with fucking drives me insane. I can't fucking handle that shit anymore. I've waited and waited. I just want my baby and my woman back home- where they belong. But, if she's back and can't even fucking talk to me... I don't know what I want anymore. What if that baby is Jake's?" My head hung, and my chest tightened. I didn't know what I was saying, I was fucking confused.

"Brother..." Hunter sat next to me and patted my shoulder.

"Nah, fuck this. Fuck her. I'm done with this shit. Over it! I don't give a shit about her anymore." I know it was the half a bottle of Jack I just polished off talking, but I was broken. I couldn't handle the pain any more.

Next thing I knew, the back door opened and Nicole was stepping inside. But she immediately stopped once she spotted me. She didn't say a word, she took a step backwards and quickly shut the door.

"What the fuck was that about?" I stood up.

"I don't know." Hunter shrugged.

"It's like once she saw me, she fucking split. Why would she do that shit? I didn't yell at her that bad the other day, did I? Nah, fucking Nicole is tough as nails. Then why would she...fucking-a Roxy is with her!" I was up and running across the room. I threw open the back door to see Nicole rushing Roxy along. Even from behind, she looked fucking sexy; waddling that ass with my baby in her.

"Roxy!" I shouted, the girls halted.

"Chase, just let us leave. You're drunk," Nicole pleaded, keeping her hand on the small of Roxy's back.

"Let me just fucking talk to her! Roxy!" I jogged up to them, immediately sobering up.

In slow motion Roxy turned around. My breath caught in my chest. She was fucking stunning, my angel here on earth. She stood there in a black maxi dress. Her large breasts even heavier, nearly spilling through her deep V-neck. Her hair, she kept long and curled, now a raven black color, setting off her olive-toned skin. Her dress had a belt with a large bow that sat perfectly on her now perfectly round belly. Her face was soft, her cheeks with a fullness from the pregnancy weight. She wore little to no makeup, Rox was perfect. I stood there staring at her, as she looked equally shocked to see me.

"Chase." My name fell off of those lips, her lips. The only lips I had thought about for the last four fucking months.

"Nicole, give us a minute," I pleaded with her. Nicole looked over to Roxy, and she nodded her head. Nicole left us, going back inside the clubhouse.

We stood there staring at each other for what seemed like forever. Her big brown eyes scanned over me. Then her hand rested on the underside of her belly, accentuating the roundness to her body. Her lips curled up as she smiled down at her belly.

"What is it?"

"Give me your hand." She didn't even wait for me to answer; she grabbed ahold of my hand and placed it on her firm belly. The warmth spread over me, like someone just jumpstarted my heart. Fuck me.

She looked completely different from the last time I remembered seeing her. She was now sporting a round basketball under her dress. Her belly wasn't riding high, more low and in front...the signs of a boy. As my copy of "What to Expect While Expecting" is now dog-eared from reading it. I'm such a pussy. Then I felt it, a strong kick in the center of my palm. My breathing hitched as I took a step closer to Rox. I knelt down on my knees. I placed my hands on either side of her belly and lowered my face to my unborn child. I kissed her belly, and I felt her hands go into my hair and she held me to her. God, her touch was enough to bring me to my fuckin' knees if I wasn't already.

I slowly stood up, cupping her face. She tensed under my touch,

4

which killed me. Cupping the back of her neck, I pulled her to my chest. Holding her felt right. She is the only one that I craved to touch for the last few months. I needed her warmth. Her small hands pushed off of my chest, those eyes looking up at my mouth. I slowly lowered my face to hers.

Roxy

THERE HE WAS, SHIT-FACED TIRED, WITH DARK CIRCLES UNDER HIS EYES, HIS SCRUFF longer than usual. Chase looked defeated. It's all because of me. I felt terrible. It confirmed my decision to stay away. I couldn't deal with hurting Chase, let alone disappointing him. It killed me. But he doesn't know that the week after I left town I went for a paternity test. They sent the results, however I haven't been able to bring myself to open the envelope. It has been burning a hole in my purse for the last four months.

Chase's rough hands cupped my jawline; I leaned into his large palm. His green eyes warmed as he gazed down at me. God, I missed him. My focus fell to his full lips. Chase started to bring his face to mine. I shouldn't, but God, my body was reacting to him. Damn pregnancy hormones and sex drive. I popped up onto my tiptoes and gently touched my lips to his.

Perfect doesn't begin to cover it. He gripped my hair at the nape of my neck as his tongue pushed its way past my lips and into my mouth. I melted into him. I tasted the liquor on his tongue as he held my mouth to his. I exhaled my breath into his lungs. I had to stop, as much as I didn't want to. This wasn't right. Even as good as it felt.

"I can't." I quickly pulled away, tears already threatening at my eyes.

"Roxy," Chase pleaded, trying to hold onto my forearms.

"I'm sorry, Chase." A sob left my lips as I saw the hurt in his eyes.

"No! You're not fucking leaving me. I just got you back." I saw Nicole and Hunter coming out of the back of the clubhouse, quickening their pace towards us.

"I have to go." I pushed at his chest, begging him to let me go.

"No!" he yelled out, grabbing the strap on my purse, causing it to

5

fall off my shoulder and onto the pavement. Hunter grabbed his shoulder, pulling him away from me. The letter from PTC (Paternity Testing Corporation) had fallen to Chase's feet. I immediately tried to squat down and retrieve it, but Chase beat me to it. Fuck. Hunter and Nicole helped me up by my elbows.

"Is this what I fucking think it is?" Chase held onto the envelope as he was still squatting on his haunches.

"Chase, please..." I pleaded with him, my hand caressing my belly, as the other rested on my lower back.

"It's unopened?" He looked up at me as he stood.

"Chase, just let it go. Let her have the letter." Oh Hunter, trying to help me out, probably not a good idea.

"No, fuck that! I have just as much right to this as she does."

"Nicole, please just get me the fuck out of here." I didn't want to talk to him anymore. I had nothing left to say to him tonight. I rubbed my forehead.

"Okay, lets go." Nicole unlocked her car and I walked away from Chase. Too upset to even get the goddamned letter back. This wasn't how coming home was supposed to be. I quickly wiped the hot tears rolling down my cheek.

CHAPTER 1

JEREMY

I WALKED OUT OF MY ROOM AT THE CLUBHOUSE, DISMISSING KENDRA. AT LEAST I think that's what her name was. As I walked to the back bar I heard Nicole's signature giggle. Fuck me. My muscles instantly tensed. I quietly walked to the doorway to spot her and Hunter as the only ones in there. I put a cigarette up to my lips.

"Give them five minutes. That's all." Nicole stated as she crossed her arms while walking up to stand in front of Hunter as he was sitting on a bar stool, leaning up against the bar top.

"Yeah, that may be five too many, sweetheart." Hunter chuckled then took a long swig of his beer. Nicole focused on the bobbing of his Adam's apple.

"Yeah, probably." She sounded hypnotized. What the fuck?

"I believe you failed to give me a proper hello." He smirked over at her and she bit her bottom lip. My fists clenched. I wasn't supposed to be giving a flying fuck about her anymore. Yet here I am standing in the shadows, like I'm freaking stalking her ass. Son of a bitch.

"Oh yeah? What kind of hello are you looking for exactly, Hunter?"

she teased while she walked up to him, nudging his knees apart, and standing in-between his thighs. He placed his beer down on the bar behind him and his hands caressed the backs of her thighs, trailing upward.

Nicole's arms came around Hunter's neck as she gave him a hug. Ha- there you go motherfucker, a fucking hug. My chest puffed with pride. Thank fuck. Next thing I knew those stunning blue eyes were on me. She stared at me silently. Knowing I was standing just a few feet away. I felt like she could see right through me.

I lit my cigarette while I turned my back on them and left. I wasn't sticking around for that shit.

Nicole

"FUCKING PUSSY!" I THOUGHT TO MYSELF, SEEING JEREMY STANDING THERE WATCHing us, and not doing shit. He really doesn't give a fuck anymore!

"You alright? You're kind of putting me in a chokehold, Nicole," Hunter laughed as he "tapped out" on my arm.

"I'm sorry." I pulled away, embarrassed. I tucked a piece of hair behind my ear.

"No need to apologize. You just need to be careful, let me find out that you're into some bondage shit." He laughed, playfully slapping the sides of my thighs. My eyebrows rose as I pulled slightly away from him. I looked down into his big brown eyes. Then it clicked- he's a little freak!

"Hunter Sabatino!" I slapped his bulging bicep.

"What?" he laughed up at me.

"You freak! Okay, five minutes is up!" I went to pull away from him, but he cupped my ass, and brought me to him. My heart skipped a beat as our bodies molded together.

"Why don't you let me show you?" His gaze dropped to my lips and his tongue darted out to wet his. I could read his mind. Good God- this man was too much. Someone needs to put him in his place, might as well be me!

"Hmm...maybe." I placed my hands on the tops of his muscular thighs and held my open mouth over his. Hunter darted his tongue out and licked my lips. Oh lord, give me strength! I quickly pulled away as he tried to complete our kiss.

"Tease!" he said as his chest shook with laughter.

"Come on, I need your muscle." I lead us out back to where I had to rescue Roxy from Chase.

Thirty minutes later...

Roxy

"WHAT THE FUCK AM I SUPPOSED TO DO NOW?" I PLEADED TO NICOLE, AS SHE PULLED into Jeremy's driveway.

"Wait, why are we here? I thought you moved out?" I looked over at her confused.

"Ugh, long story short...when I tried to move back in my apartment, my landlord had the rest of my shit in boxes sitting outside the door and the locks changed. Apparently since I was never there, they took it upon themselves to end my lease. Those fuckers! So then I had nowhere to turn except back to Captain Dickhead. I've almost saved up enough to put a deposit down on a home about ten minutes away."

"I can't believe you two coexist under the same roof. From the last I heard..." She cut me off.

"Believe me, Roxy, it has been no fucking picnic living with your brother. Let's get your pregnant ass inside and put your feet up or something." She giggled as she helped me out of the passenger side.

"I think your car got smaller. Shit, I feel like I'm birthing myself out of here." I let out a sigh as I practically rolled out of her car.

"Listen babe, your ass got bigger. My car didn't get smaller. By the way, I didn't think a preggo lady was supposed to have such a rockin' ass." Nicole smacked my booty.

"Hey Sister!" I laughed over at her as we made ourselves at home in Jeremy's house. I grabbed my cell phone.

Me: Where u at?

Jeremy: Just wrapping shit up at the club house. I'll be home in 15. U ok?

Me: Yeah, just miss my big Brother. Get ur ass home!

Jeremy: Yeah, yeah. Is what's her face there?

Me: Um, if ur referring to Nicole, then yes. And be nice to her, would you?

Jeremy: I'll see you in a minute.

Stubborn ass! I threw my phone on the bed. Being in this room reminded me of Chase after all of our "run-ins" in here. My fingertips instantly touched my lips, thinking of his kiss. My center ached. Goddamn it, that was the most action I've seen since I left Forks.

"Nic!" I yelled toward the open bedroom door.

"Yeah, babe?" she asked as she leaned on the doorframe. She was dressed for bed, hair up in a messy bun and her face freshly scrubbed.

"You know how much I love you, right?" I batted my long lashes at her.

"What do you want?" Nicole laughed, crossing her arms over her chest as she walked up to my bedside.

"Can you see if Jeremy has ice cream? I need it."

"You don't need it, you want it. Or that little bun in the oven wants it." Nicole smiled as she placed a hand on the peak of my belly. "Did you ever find out if you were having a boy or a girl?"

"No. I want to be completely surprised."

"Good. I can't wait to become an auntie. Let me see what's down there."

CHAPTER 2

JEREMY

I CUT THE ENGINE ON MY BIKE. I PROBABLY SHOULDN'T HAVE BEEN DRIVING, BUT OH fucking well. I saw Roxy's light still on, she should still be up. I took out my keys and went to unlock the door, but the door wasn't even locked. How many fucking times do I have to tell her to keep this shit locked?

I swung open the door, not realizing Nicole was in the kitchen. She jumped, losing her footing on the stool she was standing on, on her tiptoes nonetheless. Her and her short self. Instinctively my arms shot out and grabbed her, steadying her around the curve of her waist and a hand may or may have not ended up caressing her ass. Her thin tank top rose up revealing her toned stomach and the pink polka-dot boy shorts she was wearing. I fucking loved that top, usually just short enough to expose the underside curve of her ass.

"Jesus Christ, Jeremy!" She gripped my shoulders, trying to pull her shirt down over her ass and my hand on top of it.

"How many fucking time do I have to tell you to keep that door locked?" I glared down into her blue eyes. Lowering her so her tiptoes touched the floor. She slid down the front of my body. Good fucking

Lord, her tits felt fan-fucking-tastic.

"Well, apparently you need to tell me one more time. You don't have to be such a fucking asshole about it." She squinted her eyes up at me. "Maybe, if you had asked me nicely, I'd do it!" Nicole pushed off my chest.

"Yeah, just like how Hunter asked you for a 'proper hello'." I scoffed at her, walking away from her towards the refrigerator. I opened the door looking for a beer.

"Excuse me?" Nicole emphasized her words with an attitude. Where the fuck is my beer? Fucking vegetables and organic shit filling my fridge. I grabbed a bottle of Kefir, what the fuck is a probiotic? I eyed it. "Put that back!" She demanded, as she grabbed the bottle out of my hand and shoved me aside. This girl is trying my fucking patience.

"You heard me. 'What kind of hello are you looking for exactly, Hunter?'" I mimicked her in a high pitch girly voice.

"Fuck you. What the hell crawled up your ass and died? All of a sudden you have something to say? I've been living with you for what, the past four fucking months? And you've said all of twenty words to me. Then you walk in on Hunter and I doing absolutely nothing and you get your panties all in a bunch." She grabbed a beer, popped the cap and nearly threw the bottle at me, spilling the beer on my cut.

"What the fuck, Nicole?" I yelled at her. She quickly grabbed a towel and started to make her way over to me.

"I'm sorry. Shit." Nicole started to frantically blot the VP patch on my leather vest. A man's cut was his worth. She knew that she not only disrespected me, but the MC too in doing that shit, mistake or not.

"Just stop." I grabbed her by the elbows and gently pushed her back. Touching her bare skin was too fucking hard. Once I felt her smooth skin, I didn't want to stop. I quickly released her arms.

"I said I was fucking sorry." She threw the dishtowel down on the counter and grabbed the ice cream scooper out of the utensil drawer.

I looked down at my patch, fucking stained. I shook my head-fucking great.

"Why don't you just go to bed before you ruin anything else," I said as I finished my beer.

"Yeah okay, talk to me like a I'm a five year old again, and see what happens." She threatened me with the ice cream scooper, pointing it at my chest.

"I'd love to see what happens, Nicole."

"So would I, Jeremy." She dragged out my name as she aggressively attacked the tub of ice cream, getting nowhere.

"Give me that, would you? You're going to break a nail or some shit." I nudged her aside grabbing onto the ice cream scooper.

"No." She tried to yank her hand back.

"Yes." I yanked her hand back to me. Fucking stubborn ass woman. We had a full out tug-of-war with a fucking ice cream scooper. Little did I realize that whatever ice cream was left on the scoop had loosened up with every tug and pull. Sure enough that shit flew right onto Nicole's cleavage. She yelped, dropping the utensil, and shook the top of her tank top while sticking her butt out, trying to back away from the ice cream that was melting on her chest. Meanwhile, I enjoyed the free peep show of the tops of her perky breasts. Nicole suddenly stopped freaking out.

When I finally noticed that she was no longer making a scene, I looked up, my gray eyes clashing with hers. Nicole's death glare bored into me as she caught me checking out her tits. Who could blame a man for trying?

"Shit, here." I tried to play it off; I grabbed a kitchen towel and went to wipe her.

"A little late for that, don't you think?" She snatched the towel from my hands. This little smart ass...

"You know that smart ass mouth of yours is going to get you in some serious shit one of these days?" I glared down at her and her now wet tank top. Making the outline of her nipples visible through the already thin material.

"And your point?"

I shook my head as she wiped her chest.

"Nic! Are you fucking milking cows for my ice cream?" I heard Roxy shout. I chuckled.

"Coming!" Nicole yelled back up. "Thanks a lot, you asshole." She threw the towel down, grabbed a spoon from the utensil drawer and bumped it closed with her hip. I let Nicole make it halfway across the kitchen.

"Nicole."

"What?" She turned around.

"You missed a spot." I walked up to her and bent my face to the crook of her neck. My tongue darted out and I ran it along the top of her collarbone. Her breathing hitched as she froze. Letting me lap up the invisible ice cream. Her head hinged back slightly, urging me to go further. My large hand cupped her breast; I pushed it upwards to my mouth, and let my tongue drag across the warm skin of her cleavage.

"Nic!" Roxy whined, causing Nicole to jump. She quickly pushed me off of her, giving me the evil eye.

"My bad, there wasn't anything there." I laughed to myself as she stomped upstairs. I headed to bed myself, after a long cold shower. Fuck.

Roxy

I PROPPED MY SWOLLEN FEET UP ON A STACK OF PILLOWS, WITH MY BOWL OF ICE cream resting atop my mound of a belly...thinking of Chase. Goddamn it! I threw the spoon into the now empty bowl. Thinking of him made my blood pressure rise. I was stressing out and it was my first night back. This most definitely was not how it was supposed to go.

"Son of a bitch," I yelped as I felt a kick to the rib. Jeremy busted through my door two point five seconds later.

"What the fuck?" Jeremy rubbed his eyes after looking as though he was sleepwalking.

"It's nothing, just a kick." I rubbed my rib cage under my right breast.

"Well, maybe if you stop feeding that baby ice cream at one o'clock in the morn-" he was cut off by Nicole running into his back side.

"What the fuck?" he grumbled again, turning back towards her.

"Shut up! I heard Roxy. Are you okay, Mama?" She yawned.

"Ouch!" I yelped as I curled into a ball on my side.

"What?" They both said at the same time.

"Nothing. Probably Braxton Hicks."

"Who?" Jeremy yelled.

"Oh for love of God, Jeremy." Nicole pushed her way past him. She sat next to me as I tried to ride out the cramping I was experiencing.

"Jeremy?" Nicole called after my brother as he was half way out the door.

"What?" He turned and looked at her.

"Get your truck. We're taking her to the hospital. Roxy, do you have your hospital bag ready?"

"Wait. Whoa, whoa, whoa. Slow your roll. I'm not having this baby tonight!" I protested, starting to stand up.

"Look, you're a little flushed. A blood pressure check can't hurt, and by the way you're all of a sudden having these contractions, I don't want be delivering my future niece or nephew tonight in this house."

"Neither do I. I love you Roxy, but not that much. Be downstairs in five minutes." Jeremy left us to get ready.

"What the fuck? I'm not ready to have a baby tonight!" I yelled.

"Well, seeing as there is one way in, there is one way out." She had a shit-eating grin on her face.

"Oh shut up. Just you fucking wait." I poked my finger at her.

Jeremy must have been driving a hundred miles an hour all the way to the hospital, so unnecessary.

"Jesus Jer, I may have had the baby back there on the highway. We might need to go back and check." I pulled his leg.

"Ha. Ha. Ha. I just got these seats rewrapped, you better not be having that baby anywhere other than a delivery room, Roxanne." He narrowed his gray eyes at me, I rolled my eyes.

After I was situated in my room, I changed into my hospital gown. Leaving my hair down, I checked my makeup in the mirror. If I'm going to have a baby, I'm sure as hell going to look good doing it.

"Bitch, I know you're not putting on makeup to have this baby," Nicole laughed as she walked into my room.

"One, I'm not having a baby tonight. Two, hell yes."

"Just a heads up..." Nicole was cut off by the room's door opening again and Chase entered.

"Not much of a heads up, Nicole!" I glared at her. "What are you doing here?" I looked over at Chase, looking so handsome, in dark gray sweats that had the best outline of his heavy cock, a black and red Condemned Angel's MC t-shirt, and black Nike Airs. His dark hair looked fucking good with that fresh 'bed head' look. I just wanted to grab that shit. Fuck me, I am really checking him out right now.

"Nice to see you too. I'm the father of that baby, so I have a right to be here, Rox." Nicole took that as her cue to leave. Silently she left, eyeing Chase up and down before leaving the room.

I scoffed at him, while walking over to the bathroom to put my toiletry bag on the back of the toilet.

"Rox." He ran his hand through his hair.

"Chase?" I sat down on the hospital bed with my legs crossed. He dropped his overnight bag from his shoulder, and sat on the end of the bed. Chase pulled back the covers. My swollen feet and ankles were exposed. He took one foot into his lap as he began to massage. I let my head fall back against the pillow and my eyelids fluttered closed. "Oh God, that feels so good," I moaned out loud. I felt his chest vibrate with laughter, which caused my head to snap back up and my eyes focused on him.

"The letter, why didn't you open it?" His beautiful green eyes were suddenly dark and unreadable.

"I didn't want to disappoint you, the club, my father. I didn't want to be known as carrying a 'traitor's baby'," I told him truthfully, and dropped my gaze to my hands that rested on top of my belly.

"You would never disappoint me, baby." He scooted closer to me, and spread my legs apart so he could pull me closer. The motion sent chills up my spine, and he noticed. Chase's rough hands trailed up my outer thighs, and my hands grabbed onto his.

"Wait. There is a lot more of me than the last time you had your hands on me." My self-consciousness started to kick in.

"Yes, I can tell." He smirked as his eyes fell to my chest. "You're fucking beautiful, Rox." He took my chin between his thumb and pointer finger, tilting my face up to his. Chase sat up on his knees between my spread legs. I leaned back willingly, my arms holding onto the back of his biceps. He hitched my knees up, causing my butt to slide down on the bed. Chase propped himself on his forearms so he wasn't putting too much weight on me.

His mouth claimed mine, butterflies exploded in my stomach and a tingly sensation ran across my entire body. I wouldn't be surprised if we broke this hospital bed before having this baby. Oh shit, this baby!

"Chase?" I barely got out as he kissed down the side of my neck.

"Yeah, baby?"

"Press the call button."

"Why, what's wrong?" Chase immediately sat back, his dark brows knitted together.

"My water just broke." We both looked down between us.

"Oh shit." Chase scrambled off the bed.

CHAPTER 3

Eight Months Later

CHASE

I STARED INTO THOSE BRIGHT GREEN EYES OF MY SON, GIOVANNI ANTHONY DELUCA. His dark hair, green eyes, and single dimple on the side of his left cheek made him the spitting image of me; one hundred and ten percent purebred DeLuca. Roxy is still looking for a piece of her in him. But he has his mother's smile. Oh, and temperament- not sure if that's a good or bad thing.

I think back to that night in the parking lot when I first saw Rox again, that paternity letter had ruled my life. I took that shit home and set it on my dresser. That night I had that letter in my hands...it's weighed heavily on me. I'd go to open the letter- and immediately stop myself. I knew what that ink on the paper said, "Chase DeLuca you are the fucking father!" I had God on my side, and I didn't let that letter ruin me.

That day in the hospital, I confessed to Roxy that I burned the letter without opening it. As far as I was concerned that baby was mine. As soon as Gio was born into this world and put onto Roxy's chest, I saw that he was a mini me. Go fucking figure.

After the birth of our son, we went home as a family. My family. We went home, Roxy and Gio moved in with me. I made an honest man out of myself and asked Moretti for his blessing to marry his daughter. I tell you, that shit had me fucking sweating bullets; we hadn't exactly followed his desired order of things. But, Moretti was happy that Roxy was happy. He couldn't be more proud that we brought the next generation of Condemned Angels into this world.

We had a small reception down by the lake during a sunset. It was fucking perfect. Roxy was beyond beautiful that day. But damn, nothing compared to how beautiful she was bringing our son into this world.

Shit was nice and easy this summer. Roxy and Gio mean everything to me. Fuck, I look at her and see the most God damn beautiful woman I've ever seen in my life. After seeing her give birth to our baby boy, I was brought to my knees. She was a fuckin' goddess. She bounced back quickly after Gio was born; her body reaped the benefits of having a baby. Her hourglassfigure now sported those tempting childbearing hips. Good Lord. I couldn't keep my fucking hands off of her.

"Do you want Mama?" Roxy cooed at Gio while cleaning up his face after lunch. She unbuckled him from his highchair and held him to her chest. Lucky little man. Giovanni's pudgy fingers gripped her tank top at the center of her cleavage. Yeah, he has been having a hard time weaning off those bad boys. Couldn't blame him, but they're mine.

Roxy changed Gio, bringing him back to me.

"You see my new shirt, Daddy?" Roxy sang. I looked down at him; he wore a Condemned Angels onesie that had writing on the back that said, "Big Brother." My eyes shot up to Roxy, and she was beaming ear to fucking ear. Here we go!

"We're pregnant again?" I laughed while standing up with Gio in my arms.

"Yes, baby, what do you expect when you can't keep those hands to yourself?" I gave her a slow smile.

"These hands?" I pulled her to my chest, palming her ass- giving it a quick smack. "That's a two way street you're traveling down."

"True." Roxy bit her full bottom lip, before wrapping her arm around my neck, and the other around my arm holding Gio.

"I fucking love you." I kissed her hard as Gio started to clap.

JEREMY

<small>AFTER RETURNING TO THE CLUB FOR CHURCH, MY FATHER AND CHARLIE SEEMED TO BE</small> on edge this morning. This should be good.

Moretti, my father, has been the President of the Condemned Angels MC for as long as I can remember. Roxy and I grew up and into this club. Charlie, my Godfather and VP of the MC have been by my father's side for thirty plus years. We all took our seats around the large oak table.

"We have a fucking problem." Moretti let out a long breath.

"What is going on?" Chase and Hunter leaned further in on the table.

"The Devil's MC. I've been hearing shit. Ryder's brother, Jax, is back in town." The Devil's MC were right across the state line, in Sand Point, Idaho. Too fucking close to Forks if you ask me.

"So what the fuck do we do?"

"Right now, nothing. Just be on high alert. I'm sure Jax is going to be planning something for us, or me at least, seeing as though I was the one who put a bullet in his brother's head. No riding out on your own. Make sure you always have a Prospect with you. We can't afford to take any chances. Even with the patch over- our numbers are strong, but I'm not willing to lose a Brother. We will meet again soon once we have a more detailed plan of what we are going to do. Keep your eyes peeled." Moretti slammed down the gavel on the block, ending Church.

Sitting at the bar while having a midday beer, Nicole breezed right on in. Fucking wearing her workout gear. Tight ass black spandex shorts and a loose t-shirt that had the arms cut off and either sides cut out so that you could see to the bottom of her ribcage on either of her sides. She ran her hand through her long hair; her glowing tan skin was fucking screaming for me to touch it. Her sports bra was hiding part of a tattoo. What do we have here? I looked away before I found any more interest in where her tat began and ended on her body.

"Hunter, are you ready to go?" She walked up to him as the Prospect at the bar ran an appreciative glance over her toned body.

"Yeah." He quickly downed the rest of his beer.

"Where are you two headed off to?" Chase raised his eyebrow."I need a hand with some shit around the studio. New poles are going in and I need some furniture moved around. You want to help?"

"Any half naked chicks swinging around them?" I chimed in.

"Um, no," she snarled over at me. Giving me that eye roll. For fuck's sake, I wanted to see those eyes rolling back as I plowed my dick deep into her pussy.

"I can't, Nic. Roxy is off to our doctor's appointment today. I have to see how my other bambino is doing." Chase puffed out his chest, lucky bastard. If he weren't already set by having the first boy grandchild, he'd score even bigger if their second child was another boy. Should have probably been me bringing in the first grandchild, but what can I say- that shit isn't in the cards for me.

"Well, let's go then, Hunter." She put her aviator sunglasses on. Fuck me, she looked good. All the time she's been spending outside at my pool has given her a perfect glow on her skin, setting her blue eyes off.

"Alright, hold your horses." Hunter winked over at me, and started to guide Nicole out of the clubhouse with his hand on her lower back.

"Motherfucker," I mumbled under my breath. I then thought of our Church meeting and decided it was best I crash their date, I mean help keep watch of their little duo. "Hunter! Wait up." I trotted over to them.

"You in?" He beamed over at me.

"Yeah. After Church and all..." I trailed off. He gave me a knowing nod and walked Nicole to his truck. I followed in my dark gray Nissan Titan. I just put muddin' tires on her, so it was an extra hike up to the cabin.

We rode over to Nicole's studio, Dancing Bare. We hauled out furniture so that the equipment company could come in. One of the installation guys was taking a liking to Nic. He stared at her backside as she squatted down to pack up a box.

"Like what you see?" I walked up behind him and patted his shoulder. Kid looked young, early twenties. He wouldn't even know where to begin with a woman like Nicole.

"Hell fucking yes. Look at her body, hot as fuck." He nodded, while he rubbed his hands together. I could see him undressing her with his eyes and I fucking hated it. The grip I had on his shoulder tightened, to the point where I made him wince in pain.

"Do you not see the fucking cut on our backs? She's property of the Condemned Angels, I suggest you fuck off before you lose those fucking eyes. Don't ever fucking look at her again. You hear me?"

"Yeah, fuck." The young guy wriggled out of my grip and made a beeline to their truck.

"Why did you do that?" Nicole straightened her long legs and pushed her hair back over her shoulder.

"Kid was more into your ass than doing his fucking job." I looked down at her.

"Can you blame him?" She flirted, batting her long ass lashes, smirking up at me.

Before I could answer, Hunter cleared his throat. "Nicole, I have to run. Chase needs a hand. You ready to go?"

"I have to finish up some things here and test the new poles out. Jeremy, you can give me a ride back to my car at the clubhouse, right?"

"Um, yeah. That's fine." I looked at my watch then took a seat on the plush purple velvet couch. Hunter eyed me up and down, and then gave Nicole a kiss on the check.

"Call me when you get in, alright?" He moved a strand of hair out of her face.

"Yeah, I will." Nicole beamed up at him, tugging on Hunter's wrist. She stood up on her toes and gave him a quick kiss. She did that shit because I was right there. Motherfucker! I felt my jaw clench and I looked away to try and keep my temper down. I fucking told her off that day. I swore her out of my life. Of course, I never fucking listen to myself.

After Hunter left, I waited as patiently as I could for Nicole to finish up. She set up her iPhone docking station so that she could play some music. Guns N' Roses' "Paradise City" came blaring through those speakers. A smirk played on my lips as I sat up on the couch and rested my elbows on the tops of my knees.

Nicole sauntered up to the pole, and took a high grip and tugged on the pole- testing its durability. She jumped up and wrapped her legs around the pole as she spun around. Her right hand held onto the bar as her body rolled and her left arm reached up over her head and did a slow lasso motion. Nicole kicked her right leg up as her head fell backwards, splaying her hair out behind her. She repeated the same set of moves on the opposite side.

Nicole held on as she scissor- kicked her legs and spun herself around to the front of the pole. The front of her body rolled up against it. She galloped around the thick metal bar to give her enough momentum to spin around it with one hand. Swinging her legs straight out in front of her. Nicole's right knee hooked around the pole as she spun sitting up. Climbing up the pole she went, locking her legs crossed over each other, then she let go of the bar, letting her arms fall behind her. And my jeans just got tighter. I tried to discretely adjust myself on the couch.

Still hanging upside down, Nicole scooted down so that her fingertips grazed the floor. One of her feet stayed locked behind the pole as the other fell back to the floor, opening her legs into a split toward the ceiling. Good fucking God! She let her other foot come back to the floor, and she flipped her upper body up so she was sitting on her knees straddling the pole. Nicole swung her head around causing her hair to go wild. I found myself licking my lips.

She held onto the pole while getting to a standing position, she did a series of acrobatic swings. Holding her arms perpendicular to the pole, Nicole straightened out her arms while hooking one of her heels around the bar up over her head. She dropped upside down and downward, almost to the floor. Nicole untangled herself and she slowly crawled up to me on her hands and knees. Coming over to me like she was ready, ready for me to take her.

I grabbed her by the upper arms and brought her to my lap, Nicole immediately straddled me, and it felt like fucking home between her thighs. And fuck, she teased me with those fucking hips. I gripped her hips through her skintight shorts. I knew she could feel what she was doing to me, she felt the bulge in my jeans as she grinded her eager pussy onto me. The song ended and she was out of breath, her hair sticking to the side of her mouth. She moved it away with her finger and looked up into my eyes with that look. I know that look, and I've seen it many times before, the look of desire. That same look in her eyes when she told me to take her, take her virginity.

Instinctively, I pulled her further into my lap, so that her hot core was flush against my abdomen. Her small hands braced on my shoulders. Nic's small gasps encouraged me to go further,as she hasn't protested yet- and she better not either if she knows what's fucking good for her. My hands traveled up her back and gripped the nape of her neck. I pulled her face down to mine. I snaked my tongue out to lick her mouth, and Nicole held onto my jawline, while she placed two fingers on my lips.

"I think the poles are good." I felt her warm breath on my face.

"I'd say so, baby." She lowered her lips to mine, over her fingers. I felt the edge of her lips graze mine, driving me fucking wild. Gripping her hair, I pulled her face to mine and I kissed the shit out of her mouth. I wasn't taking it slow with her, it has been years since I had her under me, and I needed her there, now! I flipped Nicole underneath me on the couch; her legs falling open, which allowed me to rest my weight on her. My fingers and palms felt their way around her tight body. I thumbed her shorts, right at the crease of her ass. Sneaking my fingers in there, I came in contact with her damn panties. Pushing them aside, I brushed my fingers over her anxious cunt. A throaty moan left her lips. Teasing her entrance with the tips of my fingers, her hips rocked upwards, my girl's eager pussy. Just when I thought I had Nicole where I wanted her, was I ever fuckin' wrong.

"Jeremy...I can't, we can't." Nicole quickly pushed off my chest and struggled to get out from underneath me.

"What are you fucking talking about Nic? This isn't the first time it's happened." I sat back on the couch, and cocked my eyebrow at her.

"I know it isn't. And you damn well know how that ended up." Nicole gave me a glare as she adjusted her shorts and stood up. Goddamn, she looked good.

"That was for-fucking-ever ago, Nic. When are you going to grow up? Get past that shit, it's in the fucking past, okay?" I yelled at her.

"Have you forgotten what you told me?" Her blue eyes went sad.

"No." I ran my hand through my hair, and then I cupped my chin as I rested my elbows on the tops of my knees. I sat on the couch and watched her face and neck blush. Of course I haven't forgotten that shit. I told her I fucking loved her, and I still do.

She stood above me with her hands crossed in front of her, waiting for me to say something else, but this conversation was fucking over. Nicole grabbed her purse and I pushed off the couch to stand.

I adjusted my dick, getting ready for blue balls, and followed her as she locked up the studio.

CHAPTER 4

Nicole

GOOD LORD! I THOUGHT TO MYSELF AS I WAITED FOR JEREMY TO COME OUT TO HIS truck. The warm summer sun didn't help with cooling me down any. That was too close. I heard the lock pop up in the truck doors. I promised myself years ago that I would never feel like that for him again. After he hurt me. How can I fucking put that shit on the backburner? I damn near forgot all that shit, as I was about to spring my pussy on him like a damn moth to a flame! I went to reach for the handle but felt him behind me.

"It's a little higher than the last time you were in here." I felt his warm breath move the tiny hairs on the back of my neck. A shiver ran down my spine. Really, body? Who shivers in the summer? I felt Jeremy gently grip my hips, hauling my ass up into the cabin. His large hand palmed my ass.

"Is that necessary?" I looked over my shoulder, down at his gorgeous face.

"Was that private dance really necessary?" I felt my heart plummet into my stomach. Embarrassed, I quickly grabbed the handle and went to slam the door shut on him, but he stopped it. Before he could say something, we heard a rumble of bikes in the distance, which were getting closer by the second. I unbuckled my seatbelt, hand on the "oh shit" handle, ready to jump down, when Jeremy put his palm up to stop me.

"Jer-" He cut me off, as he listened to the revving pipes. His brows knitted together, and he seemed confused.

"Shh." He put his finger to his mouth. Right as a bike crew came barreling down the street of my studio, Jeremy quickly swung my legs around the front of the seat and slammed the truck door shut.

I watched from inside the dark tinted glass as five bikers pulled up to Jeremy, all of them were wearing Devil's MC cuts. Oh fuck. I went to scramble to help him, but Jeremy shot a half look over his shoulder, which told me to stay the fuck put.

The one who got off his bike first was quite good looking. Tall, shaggy ear-length blonde hair that was slicked back; his leather cut showed off his incredible arms and tattooed sleeves. Who was this?

"Jeremy Moretti." He threw his cigarette butt to the side as he walked up to Jeremy.

"Jax." Jeremy took his stance by my side of the truck, folding his arms in front of him. I backed further toward the center console as I saw the man eyeing the truck. Holding my breath, hoping that these tinted windows were dark enough. I felt as though he could see right through to me. "Can I help you? You're a little far from home, aren't you, boys?" Jeremy asked as he released his arms and put his hands into his front pockets.

"I think you know why we are here." Oh shit. I scrambled for my purse, but then looked up at the glove box. I opened it to find Jeremy's .45. Yes, thank you, God. I checked the clip and chamber.

"Nope, couldn't think of a reason why you're in Condemned Angel's territory." Jeremy sounded confident. He wasn't backing down. My breathing hitched when the remainder of bikers kicked their foot stands and joined Jax's side. Jax practically ran up to Jeremy.

"Ryder, that's why I'm fucking here!" Jax shouted in Jeremy's face, while his fist pounded down on the door, causing me to yelp. Jax's head snapped up above Jeremy, I slapped my hand over my mouth. Jax went to reach for the passenger door handle, but Jeremy shoved him away. Five men immediately started towards them. Jax motioned for the other men to back down, pulling a gun on Jeremy. He pointed the barrel of the gun at the same spot where he was shot before, the bullet hole still stood out on his cut.

"Looks like you already pissed someone off here." Jax pointed to the hole.

"I can't recall if it was before or after your brother was shot in the fucking head." Jax hit Jeremy across the mouth with his gun. Jeremy tackled him down to the ground. They were scrambling to get on top of one another. Fists flying. Jax had Jeremy down on his back, his white shirt fisted in his hand. Jax was throwing too many blows to Jeremy's face, and his bad shoulder. Jeremy groaned and called out in pain. Oh fuck! I kicked open the passenger door and before any of the other club members could react I put the barrel of the gun to the back of Jax's head. He froze.

I kept two hands on the grip, holding my stance. "Back the fuck up, motherfucker!"

Jax's head fell forward with laughter. "You got a bitch backing you up?"

"No, you got a bitch about to fucking empty an entire clip into your skull. So I suggest you back the fuck off him." I pressed the gun further into his hair, flush against his skull. Adrenaline was coursing through my veins.

"Alright, alright." Jax threw up his tattooed hands, and turned around. My breath caught as his handsome face looked down my body. His eyes were stunning. Piercing blue eyes. He winked and blew me a kiss. "Let's go boys. This one is in heat." Jax and his boys mounted their bikes. "We will be seeing you real soon, Moretti." They rode off. I kept my gun pointed in their direction, until I felt Jeremy's hand cover mine on top of the gun.

My chest heaved with jagged, uneven breaths.

"Relax, Nic. They're gone." He lowered the gun and took it out of my hands. Jeremy put the safety back on, and tucked the .45 into the back waistband of his jeans.

I went to say something, but my mouth wasn't working. My arms lowered to my sides and I stared down the street where the Devils' bikes were parked just seconds before. Jeremy turned me towards him by my shoulders, his mood suddenly changing.

"Do you know who the fuck you just threatened?" He roughly shook me, bringing me back to the current moment.

"What? He had you on the fucking ground, I thought he was going to fucking kill you, Jeremy, and that's all you have to say?" I looked up into his gray eyes. He was pissed.

"That's the fucking brother of the President of the Devil's MC, the same President we fucking killed to get Roxy back." He shouted in my face.

"No fucking shit!" I yelled back at him, gripped his cut and shoved him away.

"You're either stupid or fucking crazy doing that shit. You should have just stayed your ass in the fucking truck!" He pointed his hand to where the truck sat.

"Well, maybe you should have not been getting your ass beat, then I wouldn't have had to come out with fucking guns blazin'!"

"You are fucking crazy." He grabbed my wrist and started to haul me off to his truck.

"Get your fucking hands off me. You should be fucking thanking me, you asshole." I struggled against him.

"Oh, I'm the asshole now?" he smirked down at me. His bottom lip was already swollen. He spun me around and pushed me backwards so my back hit the passenger side of his truck. I leaned as far away from him as I could.

Before I could protest, Jeremy cupped my face and slammed his mouth down onto mine. I quickly pulled back from him, slapping him straight across his face. Jeremy stood above me, both of our chests heaving. I took a step up to him as he reached down to me, pulling me against him. Our mouths fused together. Jeremy moved against me, pinning me to his hard body. God, his body against mine was what I wanted and needed, so perfect. I opened my mouth to him, my hands groping at his muscular arms, pulling him closer to me. I could taste the blood from his busted lip. I tenderly licked at his swollen bottom lip.

My own groan filled both of our mouths. Good God, if we don't stop, I am going to strip him naked right here. Wait, hold the fuck up! He isn't going to get away with this shit. Abruptly, I pulled away from his face and pushed at his chest. He furrowed his thick eyebrows. I quickly turned from him and climbed in his big ass truck. That was kind of hard seeing as my lady bits were screaming at me to go back. Jeremy took a second to himself outside the truck. Adjusting the crotch of his jeans, he cursed, running his hand over his head. He then rounded the truck and drove us back to the clubhouse in silence, in an awkward, thick sexual tension kind of silence. Fucking great.

JEREMY

FUCKING TWICE! TWICE SHE PULLS AWAY FROM ME. I WON'T FUCKING PLAY THAT GAME with her. I shook my head from side to side, putting a cigarette between my lips.

"What the fuck happened to you?" Chase stood up as soon as I walked into the club.

"Devils."

"Fuck." Chase walked up to me, "what happened?"

"What does it fucking look like happened?" I pointed down at the blood on my white shirt.

"Is Nic alright? She looked shaken up when she came and got me." Chase asked as he took a seat on the leather chair in the corner of my room.

"Yeah. Let's just fucking drop it for now, okay? I need a clear mind going to Sandpoint tonight- and Nicole definitely won't fucking help with that shit."

"Well, thank God, she was there to save your sorry ass." He chuckled as he patted my shoulder and left my room. Fucker.

CHAPTER 5

HUNTER

TONIGHT, IT'S JUST NICOLE AND I. JEREMY LEFT TOWN WITH A FEW OF THE CLUB members to scope out things on the Devil's MC. I get to keep little Miss Sass company tonight. I can tell she has been holding back on me, ever since I saw her and Jeremy nearly kissing at the clubhouse after we rescued Roxy, something in me snapped. I felt protective of her. Fucking-A, we had just made out in my truck. The things that woman can do with her mouth, and that tongue ring. My dick twitched, just thinking about her round, heart-shaped ass.

Nicole had not only been holding back on me, because of Jeremy, but I feel like its prying open an oyster to get to the pearl. She's tight-lipped; something has been going on with her, ever since the accident. Maybe tonight I can coax it out of her. She needs to know Big Hunter is here for her, in every way, shape, and form. I smirked at my thoughts. This mind of mine is stuck in the gutter.

I picked up two six packs and headed over. She was making me dinner. Nicole knew how to make a man feel like a king. I bet Jeremy is kicking himself in the ass right now, having to be on that run instead of being at home with her. I walked in the back door that led to the kitchen. Nicole hadn't heard me come in, she was bee-boppin' around the kitchen singing out loud to the radio

she had playing. I admired her high ponytail and cut off shirt hanging off her shoulder, exposing her tan skin. My eyes traveled further down over her hips encased in denim booty shorts and onto her long lean legs, and right on down to her hot pink painted toes. She should know better than to leave the door unlocked, especially with Jeremy out of town.

I slowly crept up behind her and went to grab her around the waist. Nicole quickly jumped with a knife in hand, catching the blade on my forearm. She spun on her heel.

"Fuck!" I yelled, scaring her. Recognition crossed her face as she realized it was me that she just sliced the fuck open.

"Jesus Christ, Hunter! What the fuck are you doing sneaking in here like that?" She yelled back at me, quickly turning the music off and grabbing a kitchen towel. "Oh my God, are you alright?" Nicole tied the towel to my forearm.

"Christ, I wouldn't have if I knew you were going to go all samurai on me. Shit, Nic." I placed the bag of beers down on the counter and went to sit down.

"Don't ever do that again!" She ran her hand over her head and down her ponytail. Letting out a deep breath, Nicole walked out of the room, and quickly returned with a first-aid kit. "I'm sorry, I just..." she trailed off.

"No need to explain. Probably what my ass deserves for trying to sneak up on a woman in the kitchen. Especially when she's dancing her fine ass off." I wiggled my eyebrows at her. I saw her checks flush.

"Very funny. That is what you get." She looked up at me through those thick lashes. The sun has been kind to her this summer. Her beauty marks freckled along the bridge of her nose and lash line. Nicole quickly patched me up. Her soft hands lingering as she wrapped my forearm in a bandage. "Nothing life-threatening, thank God. I feel terrible."

I hooked my finger under her chin. "Don't worry, beautiful, I'll live. It takes a lot more than that to take a man like me down."

"That's not what I've heard." She giggled, while getting up and checking on the ziti she was baking. She turned towards me and leaned against the counter.

"Oh really, and what have you heard, Nicole?" I rose out of the chair and cornered her against the counter.

"Wouldn't you like to know?" Her eyebrow arched as she bit the tender flesh of her bottom lip. Reaching up with my good hand, my thumb pulled her bottom lip free. Hovering my face over hers, I leaned down to her petite frame, capturing her sweet lips.

JEREMY

FUCKING-A, I COULDN'T GET NICOLE OFF MY MIND. THE PROSPECT AND I JUST GOT TO Sandpoint and I knew that that fucker Hunter was keeping her company, in my house. We were staying the night at a local motel. I threw my bag down on the floor, lit a cigarette and dropped down on the queen-sized bed. My dumb ass just got a bright idea; I still had the hidden cameras hooked up in the house from when we were watching Roxy. That would be some shit if they still worked after all this time. I have got to keep an eye on her somehow. I opened the security app on my phone, logging in and bam- the camera images were showing on my screen.

The front door, back door, hallway, and the kitchen. There they were. Hunter had just walked in the back door and was trying to sneak up on Nicole. I watched the screen intently. Chuckling out loud when I saw Nicole caught him with the knife. Little badass. Note to self; never sneak up on her in the kitchen. I stubbed out my cigarette and got up to take a quick piss, then grabbed my phone again.

I hesitated to look again; I don't know why I was so caught up on her and Hunter. After all, I gave her the green light to go ahead with him. Even though that definitely isn't what I fucking wanted. I unlocked my phone to see Hunter pinning her up against the kitchen counter- my fucking kitchen counter, swallowing her face. I've seen enough of that shit.

"What the fuck!" I shouted and threw my phone to the foot of the bed. I ran my hand over my face and through my hair. Trying to bring my blood pressure down. I needed to get her out of my system and now. I took a long shower, changed my clothes and headed out to the nearest watering hole.

Nicole

I FELT HUNTER'S SOFT TONGUE GRAZE MY LIPS, PUSHING THEM APART. SLOWLY HE teased my tongue piercing. I do believe he has an infatuation with it. His large rough palms went under my thin shirt; his thumbs pushed the cups of my bra down and rubbed over my already erect nipples. Oh God. My knees felt weak. I wrapped my arms around his neck, straight into his thick black hair. Hunter pushed his hips between mine, forcing my legs up over his. He gripped my ass, and pulled me up onto the top of the counter. Pushing the cutting board and bread aside.

I gripped his ass and pulled him closer to me, hell, I had no shame in my game- I rolled my hips, causing friction and pressure on my clit. I was like a damn cat in heat, begging to be stroked. The oven timer went off bringing us both back to our senses- or at least myself, because Hunter was still going hard. I placed my hands on his shoulders, and gently pulled away, but he started to kiss down my neck. Oh lord.

"Hunter," I moaned as he hit that sweet spot on my neck that shot a spark straight to my pussy. I bit my lip, surprised I didn't draw blood.

"Yeah, beautiful?" he asked me between kisses. The timer sounded again.

"Dinner is ready."

"Right now?" He pulled away, giving me a sheepish grin. I barely hopped down in the little to no space between Hunter's hard body and the counter.

"Yes." I gave him a quick peck and put on oven mitts.

"Hmm, we could use those later..." He wiggled his eyebrows. I eyed the mitts, then looked back at him.

"You are into some kinky shit, aren't you?"

"I'm surprised that you haven't heard." Hunter gave my butt a swat as I bent over the oven door to retrieve my baked ziti.

"Men, so confident in how they are in bed." I threw a mitt at his chest.

"They only are when they know how to use the dick that's between their legs."

"Okay, Mr. 'I have a dick and I know how to use it, so hear me roar'." I giggled and set the table.

"Let's eat. Then dessert."

"Which is?" he said as he buttered his slice of bread.

"Me." I simply stated as I dove into my plate of pasta. I felt Hunter pause with his fork in midair, staring over at me. I gave him my best smile while taking a sip of my beer.

After we finished dinner, Hunter helped me wash dishes and we snuggled on the couch in the den to watch a movie. It has been forever since I've had a normal date with a normal guy. Someone who gives me the attention I want and need, and doesn't have a stick up his Goddamn ass all the time and treat me like a fucking yo-yo! Sorry, getting off track here.

We sat on the plush leather sofa, with my feet in his lap as we watched 'A Bronx Tale'. Classic. I felt Hunter thumb the bottom of my foot, and I tried to pull back, but he caught me by my ankle.

"Someone is ticklish." He chuckled over at me.

"Not funny, Sabatino."I toed him between the ribs. His black shirt stretched against his chest as he tried to push my foot away. "Oh, so it's a different story when someone else is trying to touch you." I giggled as he grazed his fingertips up my calves, over the sensitive skin behind my knee and onward and upward to my thighs. I tried to squirm out from underneath him, but Hunter was moving two steps ahead of me. His pointer finger hooked the crotch of my jean shorts, up one pant leg and straight across the front of my panties out to the other pant leg. He pulled me towards him.

Hunter's dark eyes looked mischievous through his thick lashes. I took off his black baseball cap that he was wearing, and flipped it around so the brim was backwards. I felt the buttons on my shorts being undone, one handed. Hmm, and he's skillful! There went those shorts.

I leaned back on the couch, letting my knees fall to the sides. My invite. His large muscular body came over me and settled between my legs. This man was gorgeous. Tattooed, broad, thick and hard. Yummy! He pushed my now damp panties to the side, finding his destination. I pushed my hips up to his hand, begging for him to touch me.

"Eager?"

"Maybe."

"I've been dying to get in this tight pussy." He groaned as he sunk his thick middle finger deep inside me. I quickly sucked in a gulp of air before throwing my head back and releasing the breath that was trapped in my lungs.

"God damn, Nic. Your little cunt is already wet for me, baby. I fucking love it." Hunter's lips came crashing down on mine. I hooked my legs around his waist, pushing my heels into his tight ass to push him further into me. All of his dirty talk was turning me on!

CHAPTER 6

HUNTER

I FELT HER SMALL FRAME SHUDDER UNDERNEATH ME. HER HEAD TIPPED BACK, exposing her long neck to me. She looked like a fucking angel, needing to get fucked hard. Seeing her dark lashes lying against her flushed cheeks drove me insane. I had to fucking get inside her, right now. I gripped the back of Nicole's knees, and pulled her off the couch with me. I carried her down the hall.

"Room?"

"Third door on the right," she mumbled inbetween kisses. I palmed her ass with one hand and I opened the door to her bedroom with my other. Once we were both in, I kicked the door shut with my heavy boot, and I took her over to the bed.

I dropped Nicole down on the cozy looking bed. She bounced and I was graced with her sweet giggle. I looked down at her, loose pony tail, shirt hanging off her shoulder, and those fucking toned ass legs that led up to her tiny panties. Fuck me. I tossed my hat to the ground, quickly followed by my shirt and jeans. She licked her lips as she eyed my tattooed arms and chest; Nicole's eyes froze at my pierced nipples. I chuckled at her, so damn cute.

Nicole quickly discarded her top, bra and panties. I was fucking speechless. I admired the killer body she had. Tits that were perky with small pink firm nipples, a tiny waist, tidy landing strip and long leans legs to lead me there. And those fucking hot pink painted toes were the cherry to top it off.

I kneeled on the bed, taking her petite foot in my large hand. I felt like fucking Hulk compared to her. She was going to be completely fucked tonight.

I brought her foot up to my mouth, and licked down the length of her foot. Nicole couldn't stop squirming and giggling.

"Close your eyes, and focus, baby," I encouraged her. And she did as she was told. She drew in a deep breath and placed one hand on her abdomen and the other released its death grip on the sheets. Slowly her eyelids drifted closed, and she was focused. I nipped the instep of her foot. Then tongued her small toes before raking my teeth along them while sucking on them. I saw her chest rise and fall as her breathing picked up.

I gently placed her foot down and kissed my way up her shin and towards her inner thighs. Naturally, her knees drifted apart. There she is, spread eagle for me. Just how she should be. An eager sounding moan came from her parted lips. Her fingers dove straight into my hair as I enclosed my mouth onto her glistening pussy. Fucking sweet, she tasted perfect.

JEREMY

"WHAT THE FUCK IS WRONG WITH YOU, JEREMY? YOU'VE BEEN FUCKING MISERABLE since we got here. Need me to bring you some pussy tonight? Might do you some good to release some of that. You know what I mean?" Bear asked me, as he slid a beer in front of me. We sat at the bar of a local pub.

"Nah, Brother, just same old shit. Hell, we both should find some good ass pussy tonight." I swallowed the cold brew. My phone vibrated in my pocket. Meaning one fucking thing. Motion detectors on the security camera were going off. I didn't even want to look at my fucking phone.

"Be back, got to take a piss." He patted my shoulder.

I was in mid sip when my phone vibrated again. I paused with my bottle to my lips. That phone was burning a hole in my pocket. I had to fucking look. Quickly, I slammed my beer down and looked at the security images. Nicole was wrapped around Hunter like a damn vice grip, and he had his fucking hands all over her.

"Son of a bitch," I yelled out load, causing a few heads to turn my way. I watched as he walked them down the upstairs hallway, and to her bedroom. As soon as the door shut to her bedroom, I knew her fucking decision had been made. Now she's fucking this piece of shit under my goddamn roof, on fucking furniture that I fucking own! She's got some fucking balls. I felt an ache in my chest; I jammed my thumb to my sternum and rubbed.

"You look like you need a good fuck," said a sweet voice over my shoulder. I glanced over to see a smoking hot blonde. She had big fucking titties encased in a black-laced halter top, with tight dark skinny jeans and some leather ankle books with a stiletto heel. She had a pretty decent face; tanned skin, bleach blond hair, too much makeup, familiar blue eyes and pouty dick sucking lips.

"Yeah, you're right about that. Let's fucking go." I threw down a couple of bills, walked over to Bear, "Brother, we're heading back to the motel. Do me a favor?"

"Sure, what's up?"

"Send Nick to go check on Nicole, at my house." He cocked his eyebrow and gave me a smirk.

"Isn't Hunter there with her?" he asked.

"Yeah, my fucking point exactly. So send him on over, would you?" I went to walk away, but stepped back to him. "Make sure he gets over there NOW." Bear knew my over protective alpha male side was King Kong pounding on his chest from the top of the Empire State Building.

"You got it." He laughed shaking his head as he was getting on the phone.

Looking at her, something about her seemed familiar. I couldn't put my finger on it. Dare I say, she reminded me of a slutty version of Nicole? I grabbed my little Barbie-look-alike.

"What was your name?" I asked her, and her lips spread into a wide smile.

"Nina, and don't worry, you'll never forget it, baby," she whispered huskily into my ear before she nipped my earlobe.

"Good." I took her back to my room, where I planned to fuck the shit out of her. Or try to fuck Nicole out of my mind.

Nicole

I LACED MY FINGERS INTO HUNTER'S THICK HAIR, AND HELD HIS FACE TO MY PUSSY. Good God, this man's tongue is lethal in bed.

"Fuck!" I moaned out as my back arched off the bed. His arms hooked around my hips and held my thighs apart. The firm tip of his strong tongue flicked my clit, and then slid down to tongue-fuck my impatient pussy.

"God, don't stop. Ever!" I looked down to admire his dedication. His cheeks perked up as he smiled against my lower lips. He stared up at me through those dark lashes. His thumb pulled my folds apart and up, exposing the ball of nerves that resided in my clit. Hunter teased the small bud, flicking faster and faster. I felt the tingling in the pit of my stomach as I felt the waves of ecstasy wash over me, making my thighs tremble. "Baby, I'm so close." Then there was the doorbell, followed by a loud "cop knock" at the front door.

"You've got to be fucking kidding me!" I threw my head back in frustration as Hunter got up, and put his briefs and jeans on.

"Don't you fucking move." He pointed a finger at me and I went limp on the bed.

HUNTER

UN-FUCKING-BELIEVABLE. JEREMY'S LITTLE PUSSY ASS REALLY SENT SOMEONE TO CHECK on her. Even though he knew she was with me.

"Who is it?" Nicole's voice sounded down the stairway.

"It's Nick!" I shouted over my shoulder. I heard the pitter-patter of her feet across the ceiling, and then a moment later she flew down the stairs in tank top and checkered pajama shorts.

"Hey, Nicole." Nick nodded his head, looking her over from head to toe.

"Nick, what's going on? Everything okay?" She sounded worried. Of course she would be fucking worried about Jeremy right now, just seconds after having me eat her out.

"Oh nothing. Just checking on things. Jeremy was pretty adamant about me getting over here to check on things, he said, 'ASAP'." Nick air quoted then put his hands in the front pockets of his jeans.

"Well, you tell Jeremy that everything is peachy here without him. And I'm not a fucking child that needs babysitting." Nicole squinted as she took a stand with her hands on her curvy hips. Nick liked that position. I cleared my throat, getting his attention off of her.

"You tell him that, plus I'm keeping a good eye and hand on her. Maybe he should take a couple extra days out there, we will need the time." I winked at Nick, patted his shoulder and showed him out.

I hope that message gets relayed ASAP, fucker.

CHAPTER 7

Nicole

AFTER JEREMY'S CUTE LITTLE SHENANIGANS LAST NIGHT, HUNTER HEADED HOME. THE next morning I was a hot mess, sexually frustrated and in need of serious release. Sure, of course, I'll take care of myself. Since I'm the only one I can count on these days. After kicking off my pajama shorts and panties, I rolled onto my stomach. I rested on my knees, sticking my ass in the air. I placed my right hand under myself, riding my own fingers until release. "At least someone can get the job done around here," I thought to myself as I grabbed a towel and padded my way to the bathroom.

I got myself ready for work tonight. Before Jeremy had left for his little trip, he was so kind to have dance cages installed at the club. They hung from the ceiling above the crowds, and tonight I was breaking one of them in. I picked my cage dancing outfit, and then my work clothes. I wasn't fucking around tonight. Tight ass leather all the way, baby. I pulled out my leather corset and skin-tight leather leggings. I put on a pair of "CFM" heels, curled my hair and did the smoldering temptress makeup for tonight. Fuck Jeremy and whatever he has planned, he can kiss my ass.

I walked into the club like I fucking owned it. Damn straight. My power walk turned the heads of the owners of the Hogs out front. My boys, Derrick, Vinny, Lucas and Conner. We all grew up together; the boys were close with Jeremy as well. Biker boys.

Derrick was the first to his feet to greet me. He was the three-piece patch holder who was Nomad. He dropped in every now and again.

"There she is." His tall 6'4" frame towered over me as he bent down to give me a kiss on the cheek. His hand slid over my leather-clad ass, giving it a firm smack. I slapped his hand away from my derriere.

"Hands!" Derrick chuckled at me; he was so damn handsome. He was solid man, solid body, solid everything. We may or may not have hooked up in the past. These boys have grown into men, the next just as jaw dropping as the last. When leather meets muscle, tattoos, facial hair, and square jaw lines- no woman's safe.

I greeted each of them, and gave them another round of beers. As I handed Conner his beer, Hunter was there perched on the bar.

"Hey gorgeous." He gave me that lopsided grin. Good God, knowing what talent that man has with his tongue made an electric shock go straight to my clit. Hunter's eyes traveled down to my thighs that were currently rubbing together. He smirked.

"Hunter." I placed my foot on the bottom shelf of the bar, and hoisted myself up and gave him a kiss. He held my chin between his thumb and forefinger, pulling downward; he forced my mouth open and deepened our kiss.

A throat cleared.

"Oh sorry, boys. Hunter this is Derrick, Vinny, Lucas and Conner. Boys, this is Hunter." My hands waived about with the introductions.

"I just wanted to say hi, I'll be around later tonight." Hunter gave me a wink and pushed off the bar. I sighed as I wiped the bar top.

"Does Jeremy know?" My head shot up to see Derrick eyeing me.

"Hunter and I are none of Jeremy's fucking business." I nipped that in the bud. Derrick's laugh rang in my ears, causing a ripple effect with the rest of them. Men.

"Yeah, yeah. We are going to head to the VIP lounge, catch you later, babe." Derrick winked at me, and I shook my head at him. I started my prep work for tonight's crowd.

JEREMY

"Wait, what the fuck is going on there? She's doing what?" I yelled into my cell phone.

"Yeah, you heard me. She was basically dry humping him on the counter. You need to get back here, Brother," Derrick stated.

I sat on the edge of the bed. "Look, I'm a little busy out here."

"Who is the fucking guy anyway?"

"One of Chase's buddies. As soon as he laid eyes on Nic, he's been sweet on her. But I have no say in that shit, Brother. I let her decide, she picked him. I moved on." My hand fisted on my kneecap.

"Well, I never thought I'd live to see the day." Derrick loved busting my balls about Nicole.

Nina crawled over to me on the bed; sitting behind me with her legs straddling my back. She massaged my shoulders while kissing my neck.

"You're all tense, baby." She kissed my earlobe.

"Well, sounds like you do have your hands full," Derrick laughed.

"Listen, do me a favor, keep eyes on her."

"Jeremy, she isn't wearing a property patch and she sure as shit isn't dressed like she belongs to anyone tonight. She's a grown ass woman who can do what she wants. But for you, yeah, I'll keep an eye on our girl." Dressed like what? Motherfucker. I can never keep clothes on that girl.

"We are heading back home. Should be there in a couple hours, I'll stop by the club."

"See you then."

I dropped the phone on the bed as I pulled my wife beater up over my head. Walking to the shower, I called for Nina to join me.

Nicole

After the prep work and the bar back stocked the bar, I went to get changed for my show tonight. It was a rave theme tonight, so I went with my all white long sleeve, one-piece leotard that had a white mesh "v" that ran between my breasts, and stopped on my pubic bone. The back was cut narrow and high, giving off an excellent view of my booty. I rubbed my tan legs with glitter lotion, sprayed a can of hairspray on my curls and grabbed my heels.

The club was packed tonight; Trina was wearing her all white rhinestone encrusted bikini. Joey, one of the security guards walked us to the cages. Derrick walked up to me, grabbing a handful of my ass and pulled me closer, but before I could protest he spoke.

"Want to have fun tonight, for old time's sake?" He yelled into my ear as I leaned into him.

I shook my head and pushed him back by his chest. He held up a small yellow smiley-faced pill. Ecstasy. We used to trip off this shit back in the day when we went clubbing when we were younger. He was my bad role model growing up. Derrick tried to help give me an escape, while Jeremy was trying to help me through my personal shit. I think that's why they always butted heads.

He placed two pills on his tongue, leaned down and kissed me. He kissed me as innocently as a biker with a dick between his legs could. I felt him pass me one of the pills between our lips; I swallowed it and was ready to go. His large palm gave me a swat on the ass and he walked back to the lounge.

Skrillex's "Promises" song came on as we loaded into the cages and were raised above the crowd. I lost myself to the song, dancing my ass off. Seducing the sea of people below me. Everyone wore white accompanied by glow sticks. I started to feel the drug's effects coming over my body. Relaxing my muscles, the room became a blur of color. The electric/dance genre songs blurred into each other.

I danced seductively, touching my body. I ran my hands up the length of my legs, over my crotch and up over my breasts. I raked my hand through my long curls, swinging my hips from side to side. The next thing I knew, my cage was being lowered to the ground. I saw the crowd below me part like the Red Sea, and who were they parting for? Jeremy. Fuck me.

CHAPTER 8

JEREMY

ONCE WE ARRIVE AT THE CLUB, I NOTICED THE CAGES WERE BEING PUT TO USE- AND the one gaining the most attention housed Nicole, basically having sex with herself up there. Motherfucker.

"Get her down!" I yelled at Joey, pointing upward at the ceiling. He did as I asked.

Nicole looked fucking hot in her skin tight leotard. Her long curly hair was now getting matted with her sweat. She held onto the bars of the cage, confused that she was heading downward. As soon as the cage was about three feet from the ground, I ripped open the door. She quickly moved away from the doorway.

"Get out!"

"No." She avoided eye contact with me, and backed herself into the furthest corner of the cage.

"Nicole! Get the fuck out, now!" I yelled out over the music. That's when I could tell she wasn't her usual self. Her pupils were dilated; she was slightly lethargic, and had flushed cheeks. "What are you on?" I remembered all too well what she was like when she used to pop pills.

She tried to bury the pain from her life at home with popping pills and getting into trouble.

"Nothing!" She lashed out at me; her dark eye makeup was smearing down her face.

"Are you fucking serious, Nic? Nothing, my ass. What did you fucking take?" I reached in the cage and grabbed her elbow, pulling her out as she fought against me. I ducked down, and put my shoulder to her stomach as I threw her over my shoulder. I immediately stormed to my office.

"Put me the fuck down, Jeremy!" She kicked her legs as she tried to prop herself up on my belt on the back of my jeans. Almost taking those shits down as I walked. Reaching my office, I kicked the door shut and plopped her down on my desk. I pushed my leather chair back as I pulled her to the edge of the desk and stood between her legs.

Nicole slapped and pushed at my chest, cursing me. Grabbing her wrists, I roughly lowered them to her lap, pinning them there with one hand.

"Fucking listen to me," I yelled at her. Nicole seemed to calm down, I wasn't sure if it was her or the drugs.

"Fuck off." I pulled her face up so I could see her. Nicole looked up at me, with an innocent face. She licked her swollen lips, letting her eyes drift close, her head tipped back slightly.

"Nic." I pushed the hair off her face, running my hands down the sides of her neck, shoulders and arms, and finally to the sides of her hips. She looked so fucking vulnerable. A small moan fell from her lips. She was enjoying my touch.

"E?"

"Mmm hmm," she hummed, her body swayed with the bass of the music that was thudding through my office. Her white leotard had become slightly opaque with her sweat; I had to fight to keep my eyes on her face.

"Derrick?"

"Does it matter? It was just for fun." That shit pissed me the fuck off.

"Fucking Derrick. Fun? Was it fun when you were overdosing on a bottle of Oxy? Was it fun when I found you on the bathroom floor, giving you CPR 'till an ambulance came so they could rush you to the hospital to get your stomach pumped? Tell me, Nicole, what is so fun about that?" I gripped her shoulders, pulled her off the desk, and slammed her back up against the nearest wall.

"Shut up!" She slapped me. I stood there quietly, and then started to shake her roughly by the shoulders, trying to get her down from the high.

I paused. "You're fucking stupid!"

"Tell me something I don't know!" She stopped fighting me. Her blue eyes went sad. "Can you let me go so I can have Hunter take me home?"

"Hunter?" I pulled my face back from hers and gave her a look of disgust.

"Yes. He cares about me. You don't. End of story. " She pushed off the wall and away from me. Nicole leaned a hand on my desk to take her heels off.

"Nicole," I started after her, mad at myself for being so rough with her. My fingertips grazed her arm.

"Don't. I have had enough of your fucking games, Jeremy." She jerked her arm away from me as if I'd burned her.

"Fucking games? You think everything is about you, don't you?" I spun her around to face me, seeing the tears pool in her eyes.

"To be honest? Yes. I. do." She jammed her small finger at my chest, and I caught it in my hand, fisting it around hers. I pulled her to me so she was flush against my body. Fucking Christ, she felt like she was made to fit me.

"Why do you have to be so fucking difficult?"

"Because you still love me." Slowly, she blinked, and then let her glazed over eyes stare up at me, reminding me that she wasn't fully herself yet. Before I knew it, she was reaching for my jaw, and I was leaning down to meet her face with mine. I felt Nicole's warm breath on my face as our lips grazed each other. Her deep breaths made her tits press against my chest. Christ, I need her. Moving over her, I caught her lips with mine. Dominating my way past her lips to her sweet tongue, and fuck, if I didn't enjoy hearing that small gasp for air before I claimed her.

There was a knock at the door before it opened. We broke apart; both of our heads faced the door.

CHAPTER 9

Nicole

"THERE YOU ARE." I HEARD A WOMAN'S VOICE. HER HEAD OF BLOND HAIR POKED through the door. My eyebrow cocked up, as I pulled away from Jeremy.

"Nina," Jeremy growled as he released me, walking towards her.

"Who the fuck is she?" Nina pushed the office door completely open.

"Don't you worry about who the fuck I am, bitch! Who the fuck are you?" I started to charge her, and then Jeremy was between us- holding us each an arm's length apart. He could only hold us off for so long. Hunter then came rushing to the office.

"Nicole." Hunter looked pissed, fists clenched, jaw set and his testosterone flaring.

"Hunter." I immediately stopped what I was doing; the high quickly wore off me.

"Yes, thank you, please come get your bitch; I just caught her all over my man!" Wait, my man? Who the hell does this bitch think she is? My head snapped back in that, "oh no, she didn't" position.

"Shut the fuck up, you cunt!" I yelled back at her, ready to fucking rip her tits off and shove them down her throat.

Just as I was mere inches from grabbing her, I was picked up and thrown over Hunter's shoulder. Jesus Christ, I have fucking legs, people.

"Put me down!" I pounded on Hunter's back as he walked me to the locker room. Once in there, he tossed me onto the black leather couch that sat along the sidewall. Gross, this was where my nephew was conceived. I immediately shot off the couch.

"What the fuck, Nicole!" Hunter yelled at me, running his hands over his head while he paced the room.

"What?" I yelled back at him.

"Are you fucking him?" Hunter stopped in his tracks, his arm motioning over to the door.

"What! Are you fucking kidding me?" I saw Hunter's muscles bulge under his tight V-neck shirt. His neck was growing red. God, he looked hot when he was pissed.

"You heard me, are you and Jeremy fucking? Because if you are..."

"No." I threw my hands on my hips.

"Then why are you in his office, alone with him? And that chick saying that shit? Do you know how that shit looks?" Hunter glared me down.

"I know it doesn't look good. He wanted to talk about Derrick giving me E tonight. He was pissed. We do have a long history. We damn near grew up together. I was at Roxy's house almost every day when we were kids. I had a lot of seriously fucked up shit going on growing up and it came to a head before I went to college and Jeremy helped me. He saved my life in more ways than one. And, before you even ask it, no, we are not, and nor have we ever fucked!" I didn't realize how riled up I was getting. My feet had brought me right up in Hunter's face. His death stare bore into my eyes; we were so close that we could have had a damn eyelash war.

Before I knew it, Hunter grabbed me by the waist, hoisting me up. I wrapped my legs around his solid torso; our lips were hungry for one another. He turned us around so my back was against the wall. He groaned into my mouth. My nails dug into his scalp and shoulders. One of his hands braced himself on the wall above my head. I squeezed my thighs tighter- holding onto him. Hunter ripped his mouth away from mine.

"If I ever," He slammed his hips into mine, making me feel his hard cock against my center. Hunter pulled away.

"Find you with him," He pumped his pelvis into mine. I gasped as he pushed the air out of my lungs. His hand on my ass drifted over the crotch of my leotard, Hunter's fingers pushing the thin fabric aside.

"And if I find out that his fucking hands have been on you," Another thrust, they were getting hard, God, it hurt, but felt so fucking good. He inserted two fingers into my eager pussy.

"I'll fucking kill him." He ground his body into mine. Rubbing the part of his jeans that covered his zipper onto my now throbbing cunt. I could feel myself growing wetter. I dropped my head back on the wall, closing my eyes and letting my mouth fall open. His thumb stroked my clit.

"And don't you ever take that E shit again, do you hear me?" Hunter nipped my neck, bringing me out of my trance. Just as I was about to climax, he withdrew his fingers. My eyes popped open and my head hinged forward.

"What the hell, Hunter?" I literally tried to hump his hand.

"Do you hear me?" His eyebrows shot up as he pinned me with his stare.

"Yes."

"Good." He reached behind his back and released my crossed ankles, causing me to immediately drop my feet to the ground. "Now, I'm taking you home. Get your shit and let's go." He walked out of the locker room and waited outside.

"Jesus, you could have at least let me cum first!" I grumbled as I grabbed the fabric at my frustrated crotch and snapped it back into place. Fucking men, always trying to make a point.

HUNTER

As I drove us home, we were completely silent. I had a million fucking things going through my head. I knew Nicole and Jeremy had a past, but I didn't realize it was that fucking extensive. I pulled up to his house. It felt so fucking wrong to be dropping her off at his house and his fucking bike was in the driveway, just fucking great.

"You've been looking for a place?" I glanced over at her as I put the truck in park.

"Yeah, I have been. I almost have enough saved to get my own place."

"Look, if you need some money..." Her small hand went up to stop me before I could proceed.

Nicole

"Hunter, I appreciate your help. But this is something I have to do myself. I've busted my ass with the dance studio and at the club so that I can get what I want. I'm almost there. Please don't take away my pride and offer me money." He simply nodded.

"Goodnight." He leaned over the center console and gently kissed me.

"Night." I smiled up at him. He stayed in the driveway until I made it in safely.

I walked into the kitchen, making sure I locked that stupid fucking door. I grabbed a glass of water, noting Jeremy's cut sitting on the kitchen table. He never left it there. Odd. I shook my head, and grabbed it. Folding it in half, then in quarters. My fingers skimmed over the bullet hole, thanks to me. Also, the hole sat right above his stained patch, also, thanks to me.

Releasing a long breath, I took the vest downstairs to the laundry room and spot treated his patch. A couple rinses and ten minutes or so later, it was good as new. Satisfied with my good work, I placed the folded cut on the kitchen table. I loaded the dishwasher, wiped the counter down and headed up for bed. As I tiptoed my way up the staircase I heard moans. Christ.

"No, he didn't!" I thought to myself. In all the time I've lived with Jeremy, he's never brought a girl home. And it better not be that bitch from the club. As soon as I reached the top of the stairs, his bedroom door opened. I froze in place. Jeremy exited the room with only a towel hanging dangerously low on his waist. In the dim lighting of the hallway I could see he had a tattoo right below his bellybutton, and his sweet v-cuts leading down to his...oh my.

Jeremy's head shot over to me as soon as he heard the floorboard creak under my bare feet. Our eyes met.

"Hey." He nodded in my direction.

"Hey." I started to make my way down the hallway.

"You all right?" His hand rested on the knot on his towel. My eyes fought to stay focused on his face.

"Just dandy." I gave him my smartass comment, as I walked past him. He quickly grabbed the crook of my elbow, turning me towards him.

"Nic," he whispered.

"Jeremy, don't forget to grab more condoms!" I heard her voice, and Jeremy winced. I grabbed Jeremy's hand by his pointer finger, and pulled him off and away from me. He leaned his head back to the ceiling and took a deep breath. My guess is he didn't want me to find out he had someone here.

"Yeah, don't forget them," I snubbed at him as I walked to my bedroom.

"What the fuck?" I heard him grunt as he slammed the bathroom door shut.

Now, I wanted to pop a squat on that fucking leather cut that I just cleaned.

I closed my bedroom door, leaning against it. I tossed my bag on the ground and quickly got changed into a pair of black boy shorts and a burned out Condemned Angels MC tank top. I climbed into bed, frustrated as fuck. Why was I letting him get the best of me? Why did I give two flying fucks about him, especially after he blew me off and has been a huge dick to me since then? If I could only let my deep rooted feelings for him go. Stupid me. God, this must be how Roxy felt with Chase. I tried to clear my mind of Jeremy as I fell asleep.

"Nic?" Roxy's panicked voice ran through the house. I felt sick, disoriented. I wanted to open my mouth to answer her, but nothing came out.

I heard loud footsteps pounding up the stairs. My body lay heavy on the cold tile of the bathroom floor.

"Nicole!" Roxy yelled down the hall, she must be in my room. The room where I found out my father had killed my mother; he found out that she had been having an affair with the President of a different MC, and that I wasn't his daughter. He wasn't my father. After he strangled my mother to death, and made her "disappear" before I got home, he

shot himself, in front of me, after his confession.

"Jeremy, the bathroom door is locked." The door handle jiggled.

"Move!" The door kicked in, and Roxy's screams and cries filled the bathroom.

Jeremy rushed over to me, checking my pulse.

"Stay with me Nicole." His voice rang in my head. My eyes rolled in the back of my head, darkness.

He had grabbed the bottle out of my hand, OxyContin. Twenty pills now were on their way to my stomach, hopefully to end my misery and pain. Jeremy performed mouth to mouth on me while Roxy dialed 9-1-1. I'm alive, because Jeremy brought me back.

CHAPTER 10

The Next Morning

Nicole

WAKING UP, I HAD THE WORST COTTONMOUTH. FUCKING DERRICK- I SHOULD KICK his ass for giving me that shit. I have been clean for years, why I decided to take that was beyond me. Blinking my eyes, I heard a thumping. What the hell? I stilled in bed, trying to make out the sound. Thump, "Oh God, Yes!" Thump, "Right there, Jeremy!", thump, thump, thump! Oh mother of God. I threw my head back, bunching my pillow up and over my ears. Just when I thought it was over, I released the tension in my muscles, then I heard it... a series of smacks. I wouldn't have pegged Jeremy for a spanker. A tingling sensation ran through my limbs and straight to my abdomen just thinking about it. This freaking vagina has a mind of its own!

An image of me bent over on Jeremy's bed while he was handing out lashes with his large calloused hand, making my ass go pink sent a zing straight to my clit. Goddamn it! As much as I hated to admit it, hearing Jeremy's grunts and groans was turning me on. Shaking the image from my mind, I closed my eyelids. Canceling the noise out of that cunt face, I slipped my hand down the front of my body. Sliding my fingers over my skin, I separated and stretched my legs out. Giving myself enough room to work with. Before I could even give a second thought to it, I licked my lips and went to work.

I felt my dampness on my fingertips, running my middle finger down the center of my wet pussy. Sliding between my folds, I fingered myself, and then spread my wetness onto my clit. I went to work on my aching nub. The louder Jeremy got, the faster I massaged my clit. Clitoral orgasms- my favorite! With my opposite hand pressed down on my abdomen, I pressed my heels deep into the bed, flexing my toes.

Just as I heard Jeremy's grunts, my orgasm came over me. My body convulsed around my own hand, my knees clenching together as I rode it out. I didn't realize the moans that escaped my own mouth. I slapped my hand over my mouth, praying to the Gods I wasn't heard.

After my muscles relaxed, I let out a satisfied breath, and scurried out of my bed. Glancing in the mirror, my cheeks were flushed and eyes a little hazy. Giggling to myself as I put my hair up in a messy bun and headed for the bathroom.

As I was walking down the hallway, Jeremy exited his bedroom, heading toward the bathroom. My eyes slowly traveled up his body. Jeremy was barefoot, a tattoo of a cross was on his right calf, and his black briefs hugged his muscular thighs. An aftershock went straight to my crotch. Clenching my inner walls, I continued my journey up over his very nicely sized package, to his deep v-cuts. Lord, my knees are going weak! I clenched my fists tightly. With a body like his, that should be a crime. Jeremy wore an intricate tattoo sleeve on his left arm, which curved up and over his muscular shoulder.

I watched his traps flex as I bit my bottom lip. His strong square chin was covered in a short, well-groomed goatee. I knew there laid a dimple so deep that I wanted to lick so badly. Finally my eyes met his gray ones, underneath his dark hair and lashes. There he was standing with a satisfied smirk on his face. Fucker. I avoided eye contact as we both were walking down the hallway from either ends, towards the bathroom.

"Nic." He slowly licked his lips. Hearing him say my name did things to a girl. Things like, making me want to rip our clothing off and jump his bones.

"Jeremy." I crossed my arms in front of me, covering my nearly exposed ta-tas that were probably visible through my burnout tank. His eyes dropped to my chest, lingering for a while, as if he had x-ray vision.

"My face is up here, you know?" His eyes shot up to mine, and he smiled. That damn smile was going to be the death of me, "By the way, thanks for the lovely wake up call. Real classy, Jer."

"Anytime, sounds like you enjoyed yourself as well." He chuckled, adjusting the band of his briefs. I swallowed hard, as my eyes dropped to where his hands were. The outline of his fading hard on was perfectly outlined in the tight material.

"Excuse me?" I tried to act dumb.

"You heard me. I heard you mewling as you were coming, all the way down here." He hitched his thumb over his shoulder towards his bedroom door.

"You must have heard that twat moaning beneath you."

"Nah, I know your moans anywhere. Sounds like someone's a little jealous." He started to walk up to me, and I stood my fucking ground.

"You wish, buddy." I pushed at his chest with my hand- God, his naked chest felt so good, firm and lickable. Jesus, focus, Nicole!

"Then prove it." Jeremy tipped his chin towards me.

"Prove what?" I arched an eyebrow at him.

"Prove that you weren't just getting your fingers wet." Jeremy backed me up against the wall.

"And, how would I do that?" My head tipped up to keep eye contact.

"Show me your hands."

"That wouldn't prove shit. You won't see anything, if I was even doing anything." I tried to tuck my hands into my armpits, but Jeremy grabbed my right wrist.

"Oh no, not see. Smell." He tightened his grip with the last word of his sentence, as if he could read my mind that I was going to attempt to pull away from him. I struggled against him, but he brought my fingers up to his nose, and inhaled. Jeremy's eyes fell closed, savoring my scent.

"Let go." I felt my cheeks burn as his eyelids flew back open and up to me. A smile spread across his handsome smug face.

"I fucking knew it." His victorious smile made butterflies explode in my stomach. I batted at his bare chest, struggling to get my wrist free.

"Fuck off!" I hissed at him. Jeremy held my gaze and he pressed his thumb into my palm, opening my fist. He kept eye contact as he put my fingers in his mouth and tongued off my own juices. I was embarrassed, but oh-fucking-well now. My body was betraying me, feeling his talented tongue move over my fingers. My knees buckled, as I tried to shove him away. Jeremy caught my flying fist, and pulled me to him. I couldn't tell you who was first to kiss the other. But I was tonguing Jeremy's mouth, right after he was just fucking some hoe bag down the hall. Realization came over me. I yanked my hand away and shoved Jeremy away from me, slapping him across his face. He laughed and sucked on his fingertips, like he had just enjoyed a scrumptious meal. Well, who needs a fresh pair of panties? Me!

"Just what I remember you tasting like, perfection." He walked past me into the bathroom. I turned to go back to my room. Slapping my palm against my forehead. Stupid, Nicole, real fucking stupid. I snatched up my towel and again headed for the bathroom, hoping that Mr. Free Sampling was done.

As I reached for the door handle on the bathroom, the door opened inward. The cunt.

"What the fuck are you doing here?" Nina stood there staring at me in disbelief, popping out her hip, clutching the towel to her fake ass tits.

"I fucking live here, what are you doing here?"

"I'm with Jeremy, if you couldn't figure that out already."

"Obviously, now get the fuck out of my way." I shoved past her.

"Don't fucking touch me." She went to lay her glossy red nails on me.

"Nina!" Jeremy yelled up the stairwell. Her hand stopped mid-air. I'm sure he was standing at the bottom of them to ensure we didn't claw each other's eyes out.

"Touch me, and I'll break you, bitch. Don't fuck with me. Just know that I'm onto you. " I slammed the door in her face after making my parting shot.

CHAPTER 11

JEREMY

AFTER MY RUN IN WITH NICOLE, I QUICKLY TOOK A PISS AND MADE MY WAY TO THE kitchen- with a big fucking grin on my face. She tends to do that to me. Why I'm trying to make her jealous with Nina, is beyond me. As I spotted my neatly folded cut on the kitchen table, the first thing that caught my eye was my now squeaky-clean patch. Fuck, Nic.

I let out a long breath. If that wasn't a way to an MC man's heart, then I don't know what the fuck is. I looked around the kitchen, spotless as usual. The entire house is always clean. My laundry is always folded and set on my bed; the house always smelling like fucking baked goods or a nice home cooked meal. You would have never guessed that a biker lived here. Chuckling to myself, I took a clean mug out of the dishwasher that I'm sure Nicole set on the four-hour delay last night. Her little habit, always yacking in my ear to conserve energy by running the washers at night. We act like a fucking married couple. Christ.

Then I heard the footsteps on the ceiling, Nicole was probably headed back to the bathroom. We should fucking talk this shit out. But with Nina here...

"What the fuck are you doing here?" I heard Nina's whiney voice.

"Oh shit." I walked to the bottom of the staircase, leaning one arm on the banister and one foot on the bottom step. Waiting for them to settle it out. As soon as the arguing stopped, I figured either they were making out or Nicole was choking Nina out. I chuckled at the latter image.

"Nina!" I called for her. Minutes later, she came downstairs dressed in one of my black t-shirts, which was now knotted on her hip bone, along with the jean cut off shorts she was wearing yesterday.

"Yes?" She put her hair up in one of those messy but cute looks. She sat at the table with a fresh cup of coffee.

"I need to head to the clubhouse, have Church. You hang out and play nice- would you?"

"Sure." She shrugged her shoulders. "Why does she live with you?" My coffee mug paused at my lips. It's too fucking early for this shit.

"She's my kid sister's best friend. We go way back, alright? She's here. She stays. Don't ask again."

"Whatever. So the clubhouse, who's all there?" Nina got up, putting her dirty mug into the kitchen sink. She is definitely no Nicole.

"Everyone. Sunday is Church days. Meeting for all of us, MC members only, no associates whatsoever."

"I see. Well, what are we waiting for?"

Heading into Church, Hunter and I were trying to enter the room at the same time, bumping shoulders. We both stared each other down. This motherfucker. I wanted to smack that stupid smirk he had right off his face.

"You get control of Blondie last night?" He smirked at me. This motherfucker had balls, sidling up next to me. He had an inch or two on me, but I definitely had him in weight.

"You know it, and maybe Nicole too since you so kindly dropped her off." I couldn't help myself. That's when the first punch was thrown. Everyone sitting at the table at Church let us duke it out for a couple of minutes before ripping us off each other.

"You fucking stay away from her," Hunter yelled, splashing my shirt with red blood.

"If she can keep her paws off me, Brother. She will always choose, come back, and rely on me. Either accept it or move the fuck on, Brother." We bumped chests.

"She isn't yours, never was and never will be."

"Why don't you let her decide that?" I wiped my busted lip, licking the blood.

"Alright, pissing war is over, let's fucking go. Take care of this shit another time, son. We have too much shit to cover." Moretti called order. Hunter and I stared each other down for a few more seconds. Adrenaline pumped through my veins. I clenched my fists at my sides, I felt as though the veins in my forearms were about to explode.

I took my seat on the other side of my father.

"Finally," Charlie laughed.

"Okay, we have shit going on. The Devil's MC is quiet, especially after your little run in, Jeremy. Too fucking quiet, if you ask me. We need to tighten security. We did have another chapter spot a few Devil three-piece patches coming over the state border. I am thinking to keep things safe; we keep everything locked up tight. So accommodate yourself for a possible lock down here. With old ladies, kids and all. We aren't going to risk anything, or anyone." Everyone nodded in unison.

My father slammed the hammer down on the block. As soon as I opened the door to leave, Nina was right there, trying to make herself look all of a sudden busy.

"What the fuck are you doing?" I gripped the back of her arm and pulled her to the side.

"I was seeing if you were done soon. I'm bored." She popped her gum.

"I don't want to ever see you by that door again. Got me?" I glared down at her.

"Sure. Do you have a room here?" Christ, could she not get enough of my dick?

"Yeah babe, let's go." I escorted her to my room at the clubhouse, passing the back bar where Nicole was serving up a few of the guys. She was leaning over the sink, cleaning glasses. Her long ponytail hung down by her neck, the tips of her hair brushing her cleavage, which was hanging all out in the tank top she wore, swinging open as she moved her arms up and down. As she raised a sudsy hand to wipe her forehead, she looked up at me. Something crossed her face. I wasn't sure if it was disappointment, hurt, or just plain pissed. Maybe all three, if that was possible. I continued down the hallway with Nina. Wishing she was Nicole.

As soon as I shut the door, Nina had ripped off her skimpy top. Her hot pink lace bra encasing her double D's soon followed. Nice. She shimmied out of her shorts and matching hot pink thong. After shrugging out of my cut, I removed the rest of my clothes, and I laid out on my bed. Nina crawled up my body, resting her knees between my legs. She sat back on her heels and bent over me, taking my dick into her mouth.

"Fuck," I groaned as she cupped my balls with one hand and fisted the shaft of my dick. I gripped her hair as I closed my eyes. Nina relaxed her throat, taking me further into her mouth. She started to hum while she found her rhythm.

"Does that feel good, baby?" She said as she paused, looking up at me from my lap. I gripped her hair and pushed her face back down.

"You know how to suck dick, I'll give you that," I chuckled, tucking my hands behind my head.

"Mmm hmm," she hummed. Shit, I was almost there, and Nina knew it too.

"Shit. Just like that."

My thighs tensed under her hands. She took me all the way down her throat, and that put me over the edge.

"Fuck, Nicole." My eyes rolling in the back of my head, starting to shoot my hot cum into her mouth, but Nina abruptly pulled away from me.

"What the fuck!" she yelled, throwing a pillow at my face. I blocked it.

"What! What do you mean, what the fuck?" I yelled at her.

"You son of a bitch!" She put her panties and bra back on.

"What the fuck did I do?" I asked, standing at the bottom of the bed, fucking pissed.

"Oh please, like you don't know?" She slid on her shorts and grabbed her top, stomping out of the room. I grabbed a pair of briefs, nearly tripping through my doorway, pulling them up.

"Nina!" I yelled after her. She put her arms through her sleeves, and aggressively pulled her tank top down. Once we were out in the common area, everyone heard us yelling and was already awaiting our arrival, Nicole being apart of the crowd.

"You fucking just called me Nicole while I was giving you head!" I halted, speechless. Oh fuck. My eyes shot over to Nicole. Her mouth hung open, and her eyes were wide.

"Ah shit. You know Nina...Nicole...they both start with N." I scratched the back of my head, shrugging, trying to play that shit off. Nina stormed off to the back bar area.

A couple catcalls rang out, I grinned and shrugged. Turning to walk back to my room, I caught Nicole's stare, her glare traveling down my torso. I knew if Nicole were even remotely interested in anything, her right eyebrow would raise up. She didn't notice me watching her as I crossed the room, her eyes following my body's every move. Come on, baby; get that eyebrow up for me. Two point five seconds later, that perfectly shaped eyebrow arched. Fucking right.

CHAPTER 12

Nicole

DID I JUST HEAR THAT RIGHT? HE SAID MY NAME, WHILE GETTING HEAD FROM another broad. What a dickhead! I didn't mean to gawk, but God has blessed said dickhead with a body like Gerard Butler in the movie 300. His tight black boxer briefs encased his cock bulge. Heaven, help me. I eyed his muscular thighs, and his tattoo "Moretti" in script along his lower abdomen. I don't know why but hearing that he said my name during sex with someone else made me want him, although I really shouldn't. Motherfucker.

"Stare much?" Jeremy yelled across the room to me.

"You fucking wish. Maybe you should have your club whores put their names on their forehead so you don't confuse them with me." He started to walk my way, and I stood my ground.

"Maybe. Maybe I like wishing it was you I was fucking." His eyes bored down into mine.

Did he just really say that? I was left speechless.

"Nicole, speechless?" He gasped as he put his hand to his mouth, all dramatic.

"Don't flatter yourself." Rolling my eyes, I went to turn away from him. He grabbed the crook of my arm.

"Ew, don't fucking touch me. I don't know where those hands have been." I stepped away, swatting his tattooed knuckles away from me, resulting in his deep chuckle.

"Unfortunately, they weren't on you, that much I do know."

"What is wrong with you?" I eyed him. He's acting funny. Oh my God, is he flirting? He eyed me up and down.

"Your top is cut too low, don't wear it at the bar anymore. You're basically giving these guys a free show." Okay, back to being a dickhead.

"Yeah, okay. I've told you before, and I'll tell you again. They are just tits, it makes no difference. They're mine to show off as I please." I crossed my arms.

"Well, someone might get the wrong impression."

"Like who?"

"Hunter." Jealous much?

"Well, I'll have you know Hunter likes my tits just fine." That did him in. He gripped my upper arm and dragged me down the hallway and toward his room. "I'm not going in there!" I held onto either side of the doorframe.

"Yes, you are. We need to talk." He pushed my arms down to my sides as he pushed my body into his room with the front of his body. I sucked in a breath as I felt his warm skin make contact with mine. My body was humming. Down, girl.

"What are we talking about exactly?" I gave him an attitude, and I tried to make my feet heavy, so he was having a difficult time forcing me into his room. I eyed the messy bed. Gross.

Jeremy hooked his arm around the front of my abdomen, and pulled me tight against his hard chest. He pushed my ponytail off my neck, and rested his lips on my earlobe. A chill ran down my spine.

"What we are going to talk about is the fact that you think you can just say and do whatever the fuck you want." His warm breath floated over my ear and neck. I could feel the tiny hairs move off my neck as he talked.

"It's my mouth, I can say what I want to. It's my body, I can do what I want with it." My eyelids drifted closed.

"No. That's where you're wrong." Jeremy's hand gripped my hip, softly but firmly pressing his fingers into my flesh.

"How so?"

"Let me show you." His lips made contact with my neck, and my knees went soft. My body slumped against his. I was under his spell. Jeremy spun me around to face him. I felt so small standing so close to his towering body. His body engulfed mine. Jeremy cupped the sides of my hips, and pulled me to him. His hardening cock was obvious as it pressed into my stomach. More like stabbing me.

"Jeremy, I...," my voice trailed off, and he cupped the side of my neck, his thumb roughly grazing my bottom lip.

"Shut up for once," Jeremy whispered as he looked down into my eyes. My hands smoothed up the front of his chiseled body. His warm skin was making me melt. My hands met at the back of his neck. Pressing up onto my tip toes as he pulled me further up his body.

"Think this is a bad idea." I finished my sentence.

"I don't give a fuck, Nic." His lips took mine. Jeremy was hungry for one thing, and it was me. A moan left the back of my throat as Jeremy's hands roamed my body. His hands caressed my backside, getting his fill. My mouth parted, allowing him access to me. He playfully licked my tongue, immediately going to my barbell. Then it was like a light bulb went off in my head. My eyes shot open, and I immediately tried to push him away.

"Wait, stop. I can't do this." I pulled back away from him. This is getting harder each and every time. God, that's hard to do when he kisses like that.

"Why not? We've been putting off the inevitable, Nic. Let's fucking do this." He pressed one hand onto his hip as the other quickly threaded through his dark hair.

"One, you just had some bitch's mouth on your cock. Two, Hunter. Three, I don't have a three yet." I fumbled with my words.

"I don't give a flying fuck about that bitch, and fuck Hunter. And, until you have a three, I'm taking the lead on this." Jeremy fisted the front of my tank top and pulled me into him, causing me to stumble into his chest. His handsome face was leaning down toward mine, my eyes closed and my chin tipped upward. Our lips fused together. Fast hard knocks sounded at Jeremy's door to his bedroom.

"What the fuck?" Jeremy pulled way from me and yelled over my head, holding onto the backs of my arms, ensuring I stayed right where I was.

The door opened and Hunter was standing there. He was leaning on the door frame, arms crossed. His eyes dropped to where Jeremy held onto me. Oh fuck.

"Nicole." He pushed off the wall and walked into Jeremy's room.

"She's busy." Jeremy's jaw ticked as he rested his hand on my lower back, pulling me tighter to him.

"I was just leaving." I said, pushing away from Jeremy, he looked down at me with a thick eyebrow cocked.

"The fuck you are." Jeremy started after me. I held up my hands to back him off and walked to Hunter's side. I saw Hunter look back over his shoulder as he guided me out of the room with his hand now on my lower back. I knew he was giving Jeremy a dirty ass look. As I always say, fucking pissing contest.

CHAPTER 13

HUNTER

I TAKE MY EYES OFF OF HER FOR ONE DAMN MINUTE, AND HE'S GOT HIS FUCKING PAWS all over her. I led her out back to a picnic table on the patio.

"We need to talk." She sat on top of the table, dangling her tiny feet. Her trademark outfit of shorts and a burnout tank was so goddamn sexy. Her ombre ponytail hung over her exposed shoulder. Nicole's blue eyes bored into mine, looking innocent as ever. Oh no, you don't.

"I know that we do." She took a deep breath as the breeze drifted by us. She swung her feet while she twisted her ponytail around her finger. Slipping my finger under her chin, I raised it up so that her baby blues met mine.

"I don't want to hurt you, Hunter." Her voice was innocent and small.

"And I don't want to be hurt, babe. Seeing you two together, makes me want to kill someone. I know I haven't claimed you as my property. But you and I, we have it all working against us. I can't even compete with him. I don't know what you have planned for yourself, but seeing as how he ranks in this MC, I won't be able to kill him." I chuckled lightly.

"So, what are you saying? You don't want me anymore?" Sadness flickered across her face.

"I think the question is, what do you think I'm saying? You saying you want your cake, and to eat it too?" I tugged on her ponytail. "It's not that I don't want you, Nicole, it takes a hell of a lot to step down to that prick, let alone to not have you."

"So that's it? Him and I, we aren't meant for each other. It doesn't make sense," she protested, hopping down from the table, looking up at me. She was a powerful little thing, and she stood her ground. I'll give Nicole that much.

"It doesn't matter if you are or not. I see you two together. It's something way deeper than what we could ever have, and you know this, somewhere in that head of yours. You were meant to be his, Nicole. Your future was already decided the minute you were friends with Roxy. He's got more than just eyes for you."

"Easy for you to say, he's the one in there with some twat. Doesn't he know how dangerous that is to bring someone from outside our territory and into this club? And the way that he has her as a fucking puppy at his heels, at his every beck and call. He's not being careful. He's thinking with the wrong head."

"Then change that shit." I tucked a loose strand of hair behind her ear.

"I'm sorry." Nicole pressed her lips together.

"Don't be. I didn't stand a chance; I was just putting off the inevitable. Doesn't mean I will stop caring for you, Nicole. If he hurts you, I'm going to kill him. But seeing the pedestal that he has you up on, that isn't going to happen. He just needs to take out the trash." That made her laugh.

"Thank you, for everything. I guess we will see what happens." She leaned up on her toes and lightly kissed my lips. Fuck, I'm going to miss her. Savoring my last kiss with her, I wrapped my arms around her lower back, pulling her up off the ground, her legs dangled down as I gave her a tight hug.

"Come on, get your stuff. I'll drop you off at the club."

I QUICKLY RAN BACK INSIDE TO GET MY BAG AND PASSED THE BACK BAR ON MY WAY back out to Hunter. I overheard Nina talking, but as I tiptoed over to the doorway I noticed she was whispering into her cupped hand over the speaker of the phone. She was trying to muffle her conversation. What the fuck is Nina up to now?

"Yes, they're all here now. Just give me a few more minutes." I stepped into the room.

"A few more minutes for what?" I draped my bag diagonally over my chest, and crossed my arms. Nina immediately ended her call. She was looking shady as shit. I narrowed my eyes at her.

"None of your fucking business, Nicole." She dragged my name out.

"Sure didn't sound like nothing to me." I started to walk up to her, sizing her up. I could take her; she was about my height without her heels.

"Don't get all bitchy because Jeremy is fucking me every day and night, and not you!" she scoffed at me, flipping her blond hair over her shoulder.

"Last I checked, he was the one calling you by my name. And first off, he wasn't either of ours. I don't see you running around here with a property patch. You're just a piece of ass right now. You won't last long here, babe. He's proving a point to me. And once I tell him about you and your little shady call, he will be onto you too."

"You won't tell him shit."

"Oh no?"

"You and I are going to make a little deal." She tucked a piece of my hair behind my ear, and I slapped her hand away.

"Why would I make a deal with you? You have nothing I want."

"That's what you think." She had a shit-eating grin on her face. Her blue eyes twinkling as she looked me over. She was up to something, and I didn't fucking like it.

"I'm not biting, you sneaky bitch. I'm going to Jeremy right now." I turned away from her and started to make my way out of the bar.

"You mean to tell me you don't want to know about our Dad?" I stopped dead in my tracks. My heart sank into my stomach. Slowly spinning on my heel. Dad? Our?

"What did you just say to me?" I watched her inspect her nails.

"You heard me, sis." Goosebumps spread across my arms.

"Sis? I'm not your Goddamn sister. You're fucking mistaken."

"Well, half -sister. Dad's alive you know, and he's always talked about your Mom and you. Apparently, those two were mailing each other love letters for years, and your Dad must have caught on, and realized you were never his daughter. Have you been so blind as to not realize how similar we look?"

"Shut up! I don't know who or what you're talking about. My Dad killed himself right in front of my face. He's the only father I ever knew of."

"I heard you found out what, five years ago?" She was circling me, like a lioness on her prey. The longer I stared at her, the more I could see the resemblance now. The same sprinkle of freckles over the bridge of her nose, the same olive skin tone. The eyes- they were the same shade of blue as mine, exactly. I shook my head, confused.

"Six." I let my arms drop to my sides.

"He wants to meet you, you know? He's always bragged about his little girl, Nicole. Broke his Goddamn heart when he found out about your Mom. He was so in love with her."

"Bullshit."

"I can take you to see him."

"Yeah, right. You're just trying to stall me from narkin' you out."

"Sure, go run along and tell Jeremy that you're the daughter of a Devil's MC member." I felt like I was going to be sick. "And that you pulled a gun on your own Brother too." Jax. Motherfucker. I shut my eyes.

"You're lying."

"Wish I was. We can go let Jeremy know together." She grabbed my hand, and I yanked it away from her.

"Fuck you! You tell anyone that I'm a daughter of a Devil, they'll fucking kill me. This MC is all I have. I'm not risking losing them." I'm definitely not risking losing Jeremy.

"Well, then you best be keeping your mouth shut, sister." She smirked and walked away from me.

What the fuck just happened? I left the clubhouse and saw Hunter waiting at his truck.

"Get me out of here, please." Hunter opened the passenger door for me. I felt sick to my fucking stomach. My world felt like it was crashing down on me. Right before we went to back out of the parking space, Moretti came running out of the back door.

"An unmarked van just busted through the front gate, let's go!" Moretti yelled. Hunter took a second for that to register in his mind, before taking action.

"Get inside!" Hunter yelled as he quickly put the truck in park and rushed us indoors. I ran ahead to Jeremy's room to find him.

As I busted through his bedroom door, Jeremy's head snapped up. He was just pulling a white tee over his head.

"We have a breech! The Devils!" We both heard Charlie yell as he ran into Jeremy's room behind me.

"What?" Jeremy quickly pulled down his shirt and grabbed his gun holster. "You get all the women to the safe room?"

"Yes, yes. Come the fuck on. We've been looking for you." Charlie grabbed Jeremy by the shoulder of his cut.

"Wait! Nicole. I don't have time to get you to where everyone is. Stay the fuck here, hide and don't make a fucking sound. Don't come out until I come for you. Do you hear me?" He firmly cupped my face, speaking quickly to me. I nodded my head. Jeremy quickly kissed me and locked me in his room. What the fuck?

I looked around Jeremy's room as my heart was racing. What the hell was going on?

CHAPTER 14

JEREMY

THE FRONT DOOR TO THE CLUB SWUNG OPEN FROM BEING SHOT UP AND KICKED IN. The Condemned Angels members were ducking down behind furniture for safety. Thank fuck, we are all here, no way a small crew could take this shit on. I heard gunshots go off in the back bar; they were closing in on us from either exit. They fucking had this shit planned out.

As Hunter and I ducked behind the same couch, my father and Charlie were shooting off rounds. Couch stuffing, wood, and debris was flying through the air in slow motion. I was able to get a good shot on the men flooding through the door. A Devils MC patch caught my attention. Fuck me. I loaded my .45 and shot a bullet through a man's calf. Every man that I saw wasn't who I wanted to see- Jax. I knew he was here for revenge.

The groups of us who were up in the front were able to back these fuckers off. The shots stopped at the entrance as Hunter took down the last Devil's MC Prospect. Out of breath, we stood over one of them who was still breathing. I flipped him on his back, pressing the hot barrel of my gun to his forehead.

"Where the fuck is Jax? " I shouted in his face. Just as I cocked back the hammer, I heard a scream pierce through the air. Both of our heads shot up, immediately looking toward the hallway to the rooms. Nicole.

I quickly glanced at Hunter and he nodded for me to go get her.

Nicole

AS SOON AS I HEARD THE FIRST GUN FIRE, I SHOT OFF THE EDGE OF JEREMY'S BED AND hid under it. I heard heavy footsteps in the hallway outside Jeremy's door. I let out a small breath as I figured it would be him. The door handle jiggled, quickly I shoved myself under Jeremy's bed, and the bedroom door was kicked in. I slapped my hand over my own mouth to keep me from screaming. Christ, I can't make a sound.

"Nina said she was in here." I heard a deep voice, Jax. My eyes went wide as I followed his boots over the threshold. A second set of boots entered after him.

"Brother, are you sure you heard your sister right?" Oh God, she was right about them being brother and sister.

"You calling her a liar?" Jax's voice boomed, and I heard a grunt as the man walking behind Jax was hit.

"Let's just find her and get the fuck on with it." With it? With what? What. The. Fuck?

I held my breath as the boot tips were right in front of my face, and then walked away. Slowly, I breathed out through my mouth. Thank God! But before I knew it, my ankles were being grabbed. I was dragged out from under the bed, kicking and screaming. I got a few kicks on the man I didn't recognize. Jax grabbed me by the wrists, picking me up like I weighed nothing, throwing me down hard on the bed. The other man scrambled to find a charger cord by Jeremy's bed, and bound my wrists together.

"Well, looks like we meet again, little sister."

"Fuck you!" I shouted, as the other man had my arms pinned above my head. Jax gave me an appreciative look. Looking at my cut off shorts and thin burnout tank, which had ridden up on my stomach. His fingertips skimmed my quivering knees, up over my jean-clad hip and circled my bellybutton. Fucking disgusting.

"If you say so, baby." Jax grinned and forced his way between my knees, bruising my thighs as I struggled against him. I could tell he was eating this shit up, sick fucker. Jax licked his lips, with a sickening grin on his face.

"Get off me!" I tried to buck my hips but it was just making matters worse. Where the fuck was Jeremy?

"I don't have much time before your man comes through that door."

"Time for what?"

"Dad wants you home. Your rightful home, with the Devil's MC. Nina and I were sent to get you."

I shook my head, "No, I'm not going anywhere with you, you son of a bitch!"

"He said you'd say that. But we got orders, baby, and I plan on taking you, in more ways than one." Jax leaned down over me, our faces so close together I could feel his warm breath on my face.

"Get the fuck off me!" I stared him straight in the face, nostrils flaring.

Jax put his gun next to my face, running the barrel over my cheekbone. My body stilled beneath his.

"Open you mouth." He tapped the barrel against my pursed lips.

"No fucking way," I said through clenched teeth, fisting my hands that were now held above my head. I could feel the cable straining against my wrists, but I didn't fucking care.

"Now, bitch!" Jax pressed his 9mm Ruger between my eyes.

Fuck. I relaxed my jaw, and obeyed his command. Slowly releasing my jaw, I opened my mouth like he requested.

"Good girl. Wider." He mimicked with his mouth as to show me exactly what he wanted.

I looked up at his blue eyes, similar to mine. Swallowing hard, and taking a deep breathe, I opened my lips further.

"Perfect, I'm sure you're going to enjoy this in that pretty mouth of yours." I breathed deep through my nostrils. I shut my eyes, expecting to feel his cock at my lips. I felt his weight shift over me. Oh, I was so wrong about the cock. The cold barrel of his gun was slipped into my mouth. Shocking me, my eyelids flew open to confirm my situation. Tears formed in my eyes as I squeezed them shut again. The taste of the gun barrel was enough to make me vomit right there. I sent up silent prayers to God, Jeremy and anyone else out there, to come save me.

"Jax!" I heard Jeremy's voice roar through the room. My eyes popped open as I went to call after him, however my mouth was fully occupied at the moment. "She has nothing to do with this, let her go. This shit is between you and me, motherfucker."

"Oh, but she does, Jeremy. You see, your father took my brother's life. Someone I loved, and I will never get back." Silence filled the room. "My Brother!" Jax shouted so loud it made me jump. God, I just found out about three siblings in the matter of an hour. God, could the sperm donor not keep it in his pants?

Jeremy kept his eyes on me as he spoke, trying to talk Jax down. "Just wait a fucking minute."

"Fuck no! I couldn't be there to save Ryder. But today, I'm feeling generous. You, you get to choose."

There was scuffling at the doorway, Moretti and Charlie were being held by two Devil's MC members.

JEREMY

"I GET TO CHOOSE WHAT?" MY STOMACH KNOTTED, FEARING THE WORST.

"You get to get decide which one you want to sacrifice. Your father and president of your MC or your woman."

"Jax, that wasn't the plan!" The other man in the room yelled out.

"I'm changing the fucking plans!" Jax yelled over his shoulder.

"Fuck you!" I shouted, raising my gun at him. The cocking of hammers on Jax's gun that was in Nicole's mouth and the gun pointed at my father's head clicked simultaneously. My eyes shot to my father, he was staring at me. I was unable to read his face. Nicole's whimpers filled my ears, I could feel my adrenaline pump as I was trying to figure out a quick plan. I wasn't backing the fuck down. No one threatens my family, my club or my girl and gets the fuck away with it.

Before I had finished my thought process, the next thing I knew, a shot was fired. And it wasn't from my gun.

As soon as that shot rang out, my eyes squeezed shut, my ears ringing. There goes my life; this is how it will end. Once I realized I was still breathing and in no pain, I slowly opened my eyes. It was in just enough time to feel the gun slip from my lips and Jax's large frame falling on top of me. Jax groaned in pain as I scrambled to push him off me.

Charlie had been the one to fire his gun. Stunning the other men holding Moretti, and the man that bound my wrists, who immediately retaliated. Everything happened so fast, it was a blur. When silence filled the room, that's when I saw them. Jeremy was kneeling on the floor next to Moretti, who was holding onto a body, and it was Charlie. My hand shot to my mouth as a sob left my lips. Jeremy immediately looked over at me with tears in his eyes. His eyes widened seeing the blood down the front of my tank top. I collapsed onto the floor by the bed, stunned. Jeremy rushed to me, grabbed my face, frantically looking me over.

"Fuck, are you alright, Nic? Are you shot? Are you alright?" I couldn't say anything. I was just in complete shock. "Nicole!" Jeremy shook me lightly.

"Yes." I held onto his shirt as he pulled my bound wrists up over his head, resting my hands around his neck. Smoothing the pad of his rough thumb across my cheekbones, he tilted my mouth up to his and he kissed me. This was unlike any kiss I'd ever experienced with him. It was full of need and desire, as if he was thanking the Gods for me. Pulling away he rested his forehead on mine. Jeremy ducked his head out from under my wrists and used a switchblade to cut the cords from my wrists. I tucked my head into his chest as I looked away from Charlie's body. He risked his life for his President, the MC, and his family. He made the decision for Jeremy, his Godson.

We both heard Jax's groan, and turned his way. Jeremy immediately got up and pointed his gun at him.

"Jeremy, no!" I put my hand on the barrel of the gun.

"What the fuck, Nic? Move your goddamned hand." He looked at me as if I was crazy. And I was.

"Please, don't. I've seen enough. Just let him go," I pleaded. We stood like that for what seemed like forever. Jeremy's grip tightened and he was flexing his muscles, and clenching his jaw.

It felt like forever, but Jeremy backed down, and I released the breath that I was holding.

"Get him out of here. I don't care what you do with him or where you put him; just get him out of my fucking sight," he told a few of the Prospects that were standing in the doorway.

Moretti ordered men in, Hunter being one of them, to help with the bodies, including our fallen VP. As we exited Jeremy's room, Moretti cupped the back of Jeremy's neck, pulling him into a tight embrace. Consoling his son, talking low enough for only him to hear. Jeremy nodded, took the inside neck of his shirt and raised it over the front of his face to wipe his tears.

"Let's go." Jeremy looked back at me, holding out his hand. I looked at it, then back up to him. What the hell did this mean for us?

CHAPTER 15

Nicole

WALKING HAND IN HAND INTO JEREMY'S HOUSE FELT...RIGHT. JEREMY SEEMED TO have a million thoughts going through his head. He was quiet. Jeremy was never quiet. Leading me to the upstairs bathroom, he opened the glass door and turned on the nozzle. Soon enough the room was clouding with steam. I leaned on the counter as I watched him walk right up to me and pull my shirt up and over my head. I stood there patiently as he undid the button and zipper on my shorts, pulling them down my legs. I held onto Jeremy's wide shoulders as I stepped out of them. Even in my bra and underwear, I felt like I had too much clothing on. I wanted him to see all of me.

Reaching behind me, he single handedly unclasped my bra, letting his fingertips trail up my back and hook the loose straps of my bra onto each of his middle fingers. His ran his thumbs over my shoulders, guiding my bra off my body. My eyes drifted closed as he tugged my bikini-styled panties down.

Jeremy took a step back from me. His hands gripped the hem of his shirt. Agonizingly slow, he peeled the shirt from his body. His tattoos, old and new were exposed to me. His detailed black and gray tattooed sleeve had my full attention. My eyesight dropped to his hands, which currently sat on his belt buckle. Jeremy's actions paused, causing me to dart my eyes up to his. A smirk played out on his lips. He knew the fucking effect he had on me when he had no clothing on.

I licked my lips, which encouraged him to drop his pants. Muscular thighs in dark gray briefs, then they were gone. Mother of God! I swear if I still had my panties on they would shoot right off my body.

Jeremy grabbed my hand and led me into the glass encased standing shower. Jeremy stepped in under the hot stream of water, his back to me as he rested his palms on the tiled wall. Letting his head hang, I watched the water trickle down his neck, over his wide tattooed shoulders and down his bare back and taut ass. He could seriously crack a walnut with those buns of steel. Biting my lip, I tiptoed my way over to him.

Placing my palms on his shoulder blades, I kissed the dip of his spine. I pressed my naked body against his, even standing behind his tall stature I felt safe. Smoothing my hands down and around his sides, I held onto his ribs, right below his pectorals as I turned my head to the side and flattened my cheek to his back. Jeremy let one of his hands drop down from the wall to hold onto where mine were interlaced over his ribcage. Tugging me to move around to the front of him, he grabbed my body wash and loofa. He cleansed away the dried blood on my chest and neck. I've never seen this side of him, gentle and broken. My heart ached for his loss.

Charlie has ridden with Moretti since I can remember. He was part of their family. I don't want to even know what this will mean for the club, or Jeremy. In knowing him, he will seek revenge. I can't lose him.

After Jeremy rinsed my hair of shampoo and conditioner, I switched spots with him. I mimicked the cleansing ritual for him, rinsing him of today's horror. The basin of the shower was running red with Charlie's blood. Turning to face me, he bent his head back to rinse. Squeegeeing his face down with the web between his thumb and pointer finger he finally looked at me. His grey eyes were brimmed pink; I wanted to take his pain away.

Popping up onto my toes, I pressed my body into his. His large frame encased me, making me feel petite and protected in his arms. He wrapped those arms around me, pressing his arousal into my abdomen.

Cupping his face, my gaze fell to his full lips. This time, I didn't wait for him; I made the move this time. I captured his bottom lip between mine. Gripping the nape of his neck, I pulled him down to me and something in Jeremy flipped like a switch. He grabbed my hair and kissed me hungrily. His aggressive side was coming out.

Forcing my mouth open, he massaged my tongue with his. The stubble on his face made my skin sensitive. I nibbled at his bottom lip, sucking on it like a damn chicken bone. Jeremy's hands slid down my backside to grip my ass. He immediately turned us to the side, pushing my back up against the cold tiled wall. I gasped from the cold. He hitched my right leg up, and bent down between my legs. On his knees in front of me, he spread my folds open to get to his destination. Jeremy latched onto my clit, causing my back to arch off the wall, and my head to fall back with a moan. He pointed his tongue to make it firm, flicking at my sensitive nub.

"Oh God," fell from my lips as I threaded my fingers through his thick hair. I pulled his face further to me. Jeremy's tongue slipped inside of me, my moans echoing off the bathroom walls. He felt my knees go weak, taking that as his cue to get up, or I was going to fall the hell over and ride his face. I pulled his face to mine so that I was licking, nibbling, and sucking my own juices off his lips and tongue.

"You like how you taste, baby?" Jeremy smirked.

"Yes. I need you to fuck me now, Jeremy," I pleaded. In a matter of seconds, the water was shut off, I was hauled out of the shower, Jeremy patted us both down with a fluffy white towel and I was thrown onto his bed. My breasts jiggled as I bounced on his bed. He quickly sheathed himself with a condom.

Nestling between my legs, Jeremy hovered over me. "Nicole?" He positioned himself at my eager entrance. I opened my legs further to him, pushing my heels into his ass but he fought to stay where he was.

"Yes?" A frustrated sigh left my lips as I tried to raise my hips up to him. His hand came forcefully down onto my hip, pressing me back into the bed.

"Today, you interfered with club business." Seriousness crossed my face, thinking back to my conversation with Nina. I gulped down the guilty taste in my mouth.

"I wasn't thinking. I just couldn't see it happen, Jeremy. Not by your hand." My voice was small, I searched his eyes to try and read him.

"What did Jax say to you before I got there?"

"I overheard him say Nina was his sister." And they both are related me too.

"Fuck. Anything else?"

"No." I broke eye contact. Okay, this is killing the mood. I don't think- no- I know Jeremy didn't believe me when I answered him. His eyes studied my face.

"I don't know why you stopped me, but I listened to you. And if you ever interfere with what I do with the club, then we're going to have some serious issues. But until then, you're getting fucked hard tonight, because I've been waiting too damn long." Jeremy quickly forced himself back between my thighs and thrust himself into me, taking me by surprise. I gasped, gripping onto his muscular forearms as I tried to quickly accommodate to him. A quick draw out and back in was just enough. My own arousal was coating the both of us.

"Oh God." I threw my head back as I felt him hit my back wall. At this moment, I didn't care about the club, Jax, or the fact that I'm a Devil's MC child. I just wanted Jeremy. We've been putting this off for too damn long, and he feels too damn good.

"Fuck, Nic!" Jeremy grunted into my ear as he hitched my legs around his toned waist, burying himself deep inside of me, grinding his pelvis bone up into my sensitive mound. Pushing against his chest, I unlocked my ankles that were around his waist.

JEREMY

"WHAT ARE YOU DOING?" I DEMANDED WHILE I WAS IN MID-THRUST. I GRABBED HER behind the knee, forcing her leg behind me.

"Let me get on top!" This girl, she was after my own heart. Let me have some fun with her.

"Hell no, I'm running this show, baby." Her cheeks flushed with frustration as she continued to push on my chest. Wiggling her right knee under my abdomen, she pushed on my right shoulder, while knocking my left arm out from underneath me, causing me to fall to my left shoulder. Nicole quickly maneuvered her strong legs so that I somehow ended up underneath her, and she was in reverse cowgirl position. Fuck me, she looked gorgeous from this angle.

She shimmied down my lap so that she straddled me mid-thigh and held onto my knees as I spread my legs as far apart as I could underneath her. Her perfectly round ass was propped, waiting for a spanking. So I took the opportunity to lay my hand firmly across her cheek, resulting in a moan and her head to fall back. Her long hair cascaded down her bare back. Well shit, if I knew she liked it like this, I would have been smacking the shit out of that ass a long time ago.

She started to work and roll her hips; leaning forward she quickly found her momentum. Nicole worked her tight pussy over my cock. Raising my head, I watched as our bodies worked together, making my dick twitch. Her hips rolled as if she were up on a pole, my pole. Gripping her ass, I pulled her down onto me as I thrust my hips upward, and I ran the pad of my thumb up the crease of her backside. Spreading her cheeks, I palmed the dimples on her back, inserting my thumb into her.

"Jeremy!" she cried out, and fuck, did it sound perfect coming from her mouth. I could feel her inner walls flex around me. Pressing my thumb further, I could feel my dick moving in and out of Nicole through her walls. That shit felt crazy. Feeling my balls drawing up, I knew I was close. Then I felt her small hand massage my balls. Shit.

"Baby, you keep that up and I'm going to fucking blow."

"Good." She peeked over her shoulder, and seeing those baby blues did me in. I held her still as I blew my load into the condom. My climax must have set her off, because next thing I knew, her pussy was convulsing around me, milking me for anything left. Her pussy was like a vice grip. She chanted a string of curses and my name as she came down.

I held onto the condom as she raised herself off of me. If she's going to be mine, I need to make sure she is protected so I can feel her with nothing between us. She headed to the bathroom to clean herself up; I followed. As we completed our nightly routines of getting ready for bed, we both were standing in the hallway; her hand went straight to her hair. I could tell what she was thinking before she even opened her mouth.

"So..." Nicole trailed off.

"So what?" I raised my eyebrow at her.

"I'll see you in the morning?" She all of a sudden turned from me and started to walk down the hall. Did she really just do that?

"Babe." Nicole paused and turned on her heel.

"Bedroom is this way." I pointed my thumb over my shoulder to my room.

"I just figured..." She looked back towards her room.

"Figured what? Get your ass in there before I put you there myself." Nicole walked up to me with her arms crossed over her chest.

"Figured I wasn't your property, so I'd sleep in my own bed," Nicole shrugged as if it were nothing. She has got some fucking balls. The mouth on her, I wanted to do so much to it. Smirking to myself, I ran my hand down the front of my face.

"Fuckin' women. Then you do what you want." Turning away from her, I almost made it to the doorway to my room.

"Well, fine then- put it like that. I might wake up in the middle of the night and want to fuck, so I'll sleep in your bed. Saves me the walk." She really just said that? Before I could even protest, she whizzed right on by me. Guess she told me.

CHAPTER 16
The Next Morning

JEREMY

WAKING UP THIS MORNING, I DIDN'T KNOW IF MY BODY WAS SORE FROM YESTERDAY'S events at the club house, or from Nicole. Damn nympho. I do believe I have met my match in bed. I felt Nicole roll over and snuggle into my side, her bare leg draping over my thigh. Fuck if this didn't feel right. I could remember all the nights with Roxy and Nicole as teenagers, having their damn sleepovers, their damn gossip and PJ parties. Yeah, I'll admit I kept an eye on Nicole. Probably a lot longer than I should have, but fuck, how could I resist her.

I thought back to that one night the girls were at a bonfire.

It was one of the first times Nicole was out since all that shit had gone down with her parents, and her overdose. Nicole's boyfriend of the time, whatever the fuck his name was, had too much to drink. He forced himself on her, ripping Nicole's shirt and bra strap in the process. As soon as Roxy called me, I rode my bike faster than the speed of light to find a mascara smeared face Nicole, holding her own hand and the dickhead on the ground. She had decked him, broke his nose and dislocated her pinky finger. She was a fighter. I was fucking proud of her, but after I dragged his ass to the bonfire pit, I grabbed the end of a log that wasn't fully engulfed and burned the back of his hands. I remember him and the surrounding people screaming for me to stop. I marked him so that every time he saw his hands, he'd think of the time he put his hands on an unwilling girl, he'd remember me, and the promise I made to him, "If you ever think, look, touch, or talk to Nicole again, I'll fucking kill you."

After that little charade, I told Roxy to head home, that I'd take care of this mess and Nic. She left without a second thought. Roxy knew better than to question me. After everyone cleared out from the campsite; there was Nicole, standing there, frozen. She stared at the blood on the dirt, she was quiet. Then those baby blues looked up at me, and I'll never forget that look in her eyes, desire. I reached down for her fist that she was clenching in her left hand.

"It's dislocated," I told her as I inspected her fingers.

"I'd rather that than something else...." She trailed off. I knew she didn't love the guy, so she must have been talking about her virginity. Thank fucking Jesus. Nicole stepped closer to me; I was still holding onto her. Quickly, I pulled her finger straight. Nicole yelped out and the tears pooled in her eyes. She clasped her hand to her chest, as she stared up at me.

"Thank you."

"Anytime." I tucked a strand of her hair behind her ear.

"Not just for tonight, Jeremy, but for everything. For saving me, Jer. I wouldn't be here if it weren't for you." Nicole lowered her hands and took a step closer to me. My breathing deepened. She was stepping into unmarked territory. This was the first time she had ever said anything about that night, which was almost a year before this conversation.

Reaching out, I cupped her soft face, and leaning down I grazed my lips against hers. Then she did it, Nicole popped up onto her tiptoes and kissed me hard. Taking me by fucking surprise, I gripped her hair and broke our connection, the both of us gasping for air.

"Nic, if you don't stop, I sure as fuck won't be able to." I clenched my jaw, praying she wouldn't stop.

"I don't want you to stop, ever." She pulled me down to her, our mouths colliding. That night, I took Nicole down to the riverfront. Under the stars, and in front of God, she gave herself to me. From that fucking *moment, Nicole was mine.*

Holding her small wrist to my chest, I ran my thumb over the bruises from where she was bound. My jaw clenched. I replayed yesterday's scene in my mind, over and over again. I could understand Charlie making my decision for me; however, my plan was just to straight up kill Jax. Plain and simple. Fuck no, I wasn't choosing between my father and Nicole.

What I couldn't wrap my brain around was how Nicole acted. This was the same girl who held him at gunpoint, was it not? And what was Jax's original plan that he mentioned? I ran my hand over her temple, smoothing her wild hair away from her angelic face. What did Jax want with her? To get to me? I'll get to the fucking bottom of this shit. Nicole doesn't need this. She's a good girl.

My cell phone was going off, Chase's name flashing across the screen. I answered it in a whisper, not wanting to wake Nicole.

"Brother?" Chase was making sure I was on the other end. I squeezed my way out from under Nicole, and slid on a pair of briefs before heading downstairs.

"Hey. I take it you two heard?" I walked into the kitchen, and started to make a pot of coffee.

"Yeah, Roxy is a mess. She's pregnant, man- I can't stand to see her like this, Jeremy. This is the last thing we fucking need."

"Fucking-A. We have the services set up for this weekend. There are a lot of chapters coming out this way to say their goodbyes. We need to be on high alert with everyone being here. I don't fucking like this shit."

"What do you mean, why such a high alert? What happened with Jax?"

"I..." I trailed off.

"You what? What did you do, Jeremy?"

"I let him go."

"You did what?" Chase shouted into the receiver. Wincing, I put the phone back to my ear.

"Hear me the fuck out."

"Hear you out? Do you know how much you're risking? The club, Roxy, your nephews, Nic, and whoever else that other girl is, if you care about her?"

"Nina apparently is Jax's sister. Jax has some other reason to be at the clubhouse, but he found Nicole first. Speaking of her, she is the reason why I couldn't do it. She wouldn't let me."

"Of all people, why would she defend him?"

"I don't know. I don't think it was so much as defending him than protecting me. Something doesn't feel right. Nicole isn't telling me something. I can tell she's fucking holding back on me."

"Well, get your shit together, we need to get to the bottom of this shit and you need to be thinking with the right head."

"Listen, I'll deal with that shit later, right now I can't rest until Jax is gone. Permanently. I don't need him hanging over this club and my family. I will not fucking allow it. After we put Charlie to rest, we ride."

"I'll catch up with you later, brother."

Hanging up the phone, I saw Nicole standing in the doorway, wearing one of my Condemned Angels shirts that I wore to the gym. The sleeves were cut off, and the open sides exposed the curvature of her hips. Her long amazon-woman hair made her look fuckable. I thought by the way she rode my cock last night that shit would have broken off in her. Palming my groin, I saw her biting her bottom lip, as she read my mind. Sauntering up to me, Nicole hooked her pointer finger, motioning for me to come forward.

"Promise me something?"

"Anything." I gripped her ass, brining her to me.

"Please, leave it alone, Jeremy." I stepped back from her.

"What did I fucking say last night? It's MC business, Nicole, something that doesn't involve you. You're not my property- so whatever is going through your mind, forget it. God, you're just as nosey as that bitch, Nina." I shook my head, turning around- placing my palms on the sink.

"What did you just fucking say to me?" Okay, maybe that was a little harsh, but shit, Nicole needed to back the fuck off.

"You heard me, Nicole. Stay the fuck out of it. I don't know how else to get it through that skull of yours." Next thing I knew, Nicole pulled me around by my arm and I caught a right hook on my chin. She ripped my shirt off her body, balled it up, and shoved it against my chest.

"Fuck you, Jeremy!" She turned her back to me, walking away, wearing nothing but a pair of sheer cheeky panties. Rubbing my chin where she just decked me, I felt my dick jump. I think I'm in fucking love.

"You already did!" I yelled after her.

Nicole

MOTHERFUCKER! I COULDN'T BELIEVE HE JUST COMPARED ME TO HER. SLAMMING THE door shut to the bathroom, I shimmied out of my panties and walked into the shower. Images of us from yesterday flashed through my mind. Furious at Jeremy, I grabbed my razor and cream. Quickly lathering my leg, I quickly shaved my legs. Just as I pumped more shaving cream into my palm, I felt a breeze. Trying to ignore him, I went about what I was doing. I felt him against my back.

"Fuck off, Jeremy."

"Babe, you need to check yourself. If you're going to be mine, you need to fucking respect me." This made me laugh out loud.

"Yours? So, now you want me? Scared of actually having an Old Lady who

won't take shit and tell you how it really is without candy coating your dick?" I spun around to him and poked my finger into his muscular pectoral. The shaving cream slid off my wet hand onto his chest, and away with the stream of water. Sweet Jesus, why do men look better when you're mad at them?

"You keep poking me with that finger, I'm going to find a new home for it." I cocked my eyebrow up.

Before I could protest, Jeremy took my razor from me, turning me back around, as he pressed himself to my backside. Taking my right hand into his, he guided my hand down the front of my body. Jeremy's left hand came up and cupped my left breast, thumbing my nipple. It pebbled immediately under his touch. I pushed my ass back into him, feeling his hardening cock against my lower back. A groan at my earlobe encouraged me to push harder against him.

Our hands drifted together towards my aching center. Of course I was ready for him. As I cupped my own mound, he extended my fingers lower, overlapping his middle finger over mine. Bending over me, he bent his knees to get leverage. Guiding both of our fingers inside of me. My head fell back onto his shoulder. Jeremy kissed that sweet spot on my neck, causing my knees to go weak, and butterflies to bloom in my lower abdomen. As he moved our hands together I rotated my hips against him.

"Nice and wet for me, baby. How you should always be." Removing both our hands, Jeremy gripped my hair, forcing me to bend forward. Bracing my fingertips on the built-in seat, I rose up onto my tiptoes, allowing him the perfect angle. Hard and fast was Jeremy's pace this morning, and fuck no, I didn't mind. Jeremy dug his fingertips into my hips as he pounded his way into me. Water splashed down my back and over my shoulders, my sopping wet hair swung back and forth with Jeremy's rhythm.

"Right there," He grunted as I felt him swell inside me. My knuckles turned white from my death grip. Christ, the man could fuck. Looking between my legs, I saw Jeremy go up on his tip-toes, I knew he was there. Pushing my ass into him, I felt him pull me into him as he held still, emptying himself into me. Feeling the warm liquid seep down my leg as Jeremy pulled out of me. I felt empty without him. After I straightened my back, Jeremy was filling his hand with my shaving cream.

"What are you doing?" I tilted my head back under the showerhead.

"Just shut up and turn around." His empty hand spun my back to his chest. He smoothed the cream onto the flesh above my pussy. Delicately he shaved me, such an intimate gesture that he was showing me. Who knew the big bad biker had a soft side? I peeked over my shoulder to see him in deep

concentration. So fucking cute, I cupped the side of his head and gave him a tiny peck on the side of his chin, resulting in a side smirk. Holding in my squeal, I bit my lip and allowed him to finish.

CHAPTER 17
Two Days Later

JEREMY

SHIT AROUND THE CLUBHOUSE HAS BEEN FUCKING WEIRD WITHOUT CHARLIE HERE. Rumors of my Dad making me VP have been flying around here. I'd be honored for the spot, to honor Charlie. Today we had a couple chapters in from surrounding areas. Charlie's burial was today. Nicole was down the hall getting ready; I looked at myself in the mirror as I buttoned up a black shirt. Looking at my tattooed knuckles that read "Condemned" when I placed my fists together. Becoming a member of this club was all I wanted as a kid. Watching my Dad be President of the Condemned Angels did things to a kid. I would ride around on my battery operated Yamaha Raptor, until I could go to the Little Rider, which resembled a Spyder.

My Ma, God rest her soul, even made me a mini cut. Riding around with my Mohawk, rolled up bandana around my lower face, I was a badass little fucker. I could only hope that my son would want this as bad as I did, and still do. If I do become VP of this club, shit will change. Things have never been that violent with the club. With the Devils threatening my club and family, shit will change. I refuse to lose another

Brother. The first motherfucker on my list is Jax Gallo.

I heard a small knock at my door, Nicole. Christ, she looked beautiful. She wore a skintight black dress, with a deep v in the front and back, ruched sides that hugged her curves and ended mid-thigh. She wore some black wedged heels. Her long hair was loosely curled, my favorite. She was naturally beautiful and didn't need any of that extra war paint to make her look good. Walking up to me, she avoided eye contact and fixed the collar on my shirt. Her sweet perfume wafted over me. Nicole's focus drifted up to my mouth, then her blue eyes pierced mine. I caressed her bare shoulders. She knew I had a shit load going on inside my head, but something about her seemed off.

I pulled Nicole closer to me. I slid my hands to the nape of her neck, and I kissed her mouth. Nipping her full bottom lip, a small sigh left her mouth. I needed her today, whether she knew it or not.

"Let's go, before I tie you to the bed." Making me smile, she placed her hands over mine.

We went to the service on the outskirts of town. The line of hogs and choppers was almost a mile long. We all followed the hearse, taking one last ride with our fallen brother. As touching as that shit was, it was hard as fuck saying goodbye to my Godfather. Charlie was there for every birthday party, graduation, and holiday. We were his family and he was ours.

Arriving at the cemetery, we huddled around Charlie's plot. I watched my Dad, as he was getting ready to start his speech, he immediately broke down. Charlie had helped my father through the toughest time in in his life, losing Ma. Getting him through that shit, helping take care of Roxy and I, helping with the club. Everything that Charlie has done will never be forgotten. I owed so much to Charlie, now I wont be able to thank him. Dad pulled himself together to give his thanks and farewells to his Brother.

Feeling a small hand slide into my palm, I looked to my left to see Roxy. Her red-rimmed eyes looked up at mine. Pulling her to my side, we said goodbye to Charlie together. Her hand caressed her small baby bump, I felt her squeeze my hand.

"Jer?" Tugging on the bottom of my shirt to get my attention, the same exact way she did when she was a kid.

"Yea, Rox?"

"We're going to name him Charlie." An ache pinged inside my chest.

I pulled Roxy into a hug, kissing her temple. I'd do anything for my sister. The one weakness I have; the women in my life.

"Promise me, you'll kill them." Roxy's request was low enough for only me to hear. Fuck me. Having a request from my sister to kill them, and another request from my girl, to let them be. What the fuck?

"I promise, Rox. They'll fucking pay for this shit." I smoothed her long hair. I peeked over her head to see Chase and Nicole standing together. My brother was consoling Nicole- his arm around her shoulder. I could tell she was trying to hold it in. Christ, she's only human, and a chick at that. She's going to be fucking pissed when she finds out my decision.

Before lowering Charlie's casket into the ground, Dad placed a Condemned Angels cut on top. We all walked up individually to lay roses over him. At the end of the ceremony, we all rode out. In one big group of about seventy bikes, we rode out to the clubhouse.

Nicole

I TOOK A SEAT ON THE BACK PICNIC TABLE, KICKING OFF MY WEDGED HEELS AND placing them next to me on top of the table. Flashes of today still weighed heavily on my mind. Letting my feet dangle off the edge, all I could think of was that it could have been Jeremy in that casket. Stilling my feet, I felt my stomach knot up, and my shoulders shake. Trying to hold it together, I held onto my stomach, letting my sobs loose.

"Babe?" I looked up and saw Jeremy's figure outlined by the sunlight. He tossed his cigarette butt on the ground. His voice startled me, and I quickly wiped away the escaping tears. Avoiding eye contact, I licked my dry lips.

"How long have you been standing there?"

"Long enough." He stood in front of me in his change of clothes. Black riding boots, dark blue jeans, a black thermal pushed up onto his forearms, exposing his intricately patterned tattoos. His cut hung open over his broad chest. The scruff on his square jaw had darkened; the bags under his beautiful gray eyes were prominent. He looked worn down. Jeremy blew out the cloud of smoke he held in his lungs above my head.

"You know I hate that shit." I leaned back on my hands.

Pushing the hem of my skirt up onto my upper thighs, Jeremy forced my knees apart, making his way between them. Kneading my thigh muscles, his legs were flush with the edge of the table.

"And you know I hate when you keep shit from me." My swinging legs paused momentarily, "Don't even think that I haven't noticed over the past few days that you've been distant with me." He pushed my hair over my shoulder.

"Fuck Jeremy, why wouldn't I be? Jesus, that could be have been you!" I yelled up at him. Pushing at his chest.

Grabbing my wrists, he pinned them to my sides. "Calm the fuck down, would you?"

"You could have died!" Stupid tears rolled down my face. Jeremy cupped my face, rubbing my wet cheeks with his thumbs.

"But I didn't." He gripped the back of my head, forcing his mouth onto mine. He tasted like cigarettes and whiskey. Too stubborn to let him take control of this conversation, I fisted the lapels of his cut, trying to push him away while ripping my mouth from his. Every move I made, Jeremy anticipated. Even blocking my right hand from smacking his face. "I didn't die, Nicole." he said, while looking deep into my eyes and I couldn't look away from him. I couldn't ignore that electrical current that I felt when he touched me. His touch made my skin burn, in the most delicious way. Spreading my legs wider, I heeled the back of his legs with my bare feet, pulling him into me.

"Then show me you didn't," I dared him.

Gripping my hips, Jeremy pulled me up off the picnic table. My legs tightened around his waist. He supported my weight by palming my ass as I wrapped my arms around his neck. Gripping his hair between my fingers, he pulled his mouth from mine, sucking the air through his teeth.

"Jeremy, I need you. Right fucking now, and down the road too. Promise me you won't go looking for revenge?" He said nothing. Frantically I searched his eyes, no emotion. "Fucking promise me, Jeremy!" I slid down his body, and he didn't fight me.

"I can't promise you that." His jaw tightened and he looked over my head.

"Then you're obviously not the man I thought you were. You don't give a shit about me. It'll always be you and your MC. Risking your life! You're going to risk losing me? Risk the chance of us ever being anything? Are you that fucking selfish?" I pushed away from him, grabbing my shoes and clutch.

As I tried to walk past him, Jeremy grabbed my upper arm.

"It's not like that, and you fucking know it. You mean something to me, Nic."

"Yeah, fucking right." I walked away from him, towards my car.

I knew then and there what I had to do. I had to get to the Devils before Jeremy did.

CHAPTER 18

Later That Night

JEREMY

CHASE BACKED OUT OF MY DRIVEWAY, DROPPING ME OFF SO I DIDN'T RIDE HOME WAS a good idea of his, not letting me ride home on my own. I stumbled to the back door. I was about to use my key when I realized Nicole's car was in the driveway. I figured she came home after our little confrontation earlier. I didn't think she'd be home after that, more like staying the night at Chase and Roxy's house. I went to open the door handle, locked. That's unlike her. She never locks this damn door, no matter how many times I bitch at her.

Jingling my keys in my left hand, I found the house key and walked into a dark kitchen. The house was quiet, Nic was probably sleeping. The dim hallway light led my way to the staircase. Slowly climbing the stairs-more like up one down two, railing, wall, repeat. I saw her bedroom door cracked, with light spilling out. Swallowing my pride, I went to confront her. Knocking lightly on her door, there wasn't an answer; maybe she fell asleep with the light on. Splaying my fingers on the door, I pushed it open to see her in bed with the covers around her like a damn cocoon.

Feeling guilty about earlier, I rubbed the back of my neck and sat on the edge of her bed.

"Nic, baby." I gently shook her with a hand on her hip.

Stirring, she moved the covers down.

"Hey, sexy." Nina sat up, removing the covers from herself. I shot off the bed, reaching for my gun holster.

"Don't even think about it." Freezing my hands as I felt the cold metal against my temple. Looking out of the corner of my eye, I saw someone I didn't expect to see holding a gun to my head- Nicole.

What the fuck? Taking a deep breath, and clenching my cheeks, I looked over her shoulder to see Jax propped against the wall. He had his arm in a sling, and a shit-eating grin.

My eyes looked down at Nicole. Her eyes were unreadable. I spotted her packed bags in the corner of the room. Nina got out of Nicole's bed, adjusting her tight Harley Davidson halter-top.

"Should have killed you when I had the fucking chance," I spat out at Jax, ignoring Nicole.

"Well, we have our little sister to thank for that, right, little Nikki?" My eyes flashed to her, Nicole's eyelids shut hard, then opened back up to me.

"What the fuck are they talking about, Nic?" I yelled at her, she barely flinched.

"You just couldn't fucking listen to me, could you? I couldn't let you do it! You couldn't fucking promise me shit, so I took matters into my own hands. Before the ambush at the club, I found out that Nina is my sister and Jax..." Her small voice trailed off.

"Your brother? You were protecting them? I bet you knew all along. You fucking bitch!" I spat at Nicole. Looking between her and Nina, I was starting to see the slight resemblance. Fuck, how could I have missed it?

"Shut up!"Jax's voice boomed over ours, causing all eyes in the room to go to him.

"Now, Jeremy, you should be fucking thanking her. She's taking the debt with the Condemned Angels onto her own shoulders. She loves you too much to let anything bad happen to you." Now shit was fucking making sense.

"No, she fucking isn't going anywhere with you, crazy ass motherfucker!" I yelled at them. Nina suddenly grabbed Nicole by her long hair, she yelped out, while reaching back and grabbing onto Nina's hand.

"Get the fuck off me!" Nicole yelled over her shoulder. I stepped towards her, and Nina raised a gun at me, and Jax walked up behind Nicole- wrapping his arm around her waist under her breasts. My fists clenched at my sides.

"Fuck off, she's ours now. She always has been...seeing as her real Dad is a part of Devil's MC. She's never been apart of you or your club. Now, we're taking her home." Jax kept eye contact while shoving his nose into Nicole's hair, and breathing deep. Motherfucker!

"You won't even make it out of town," I threatened him.

"We'll see. I'm sure they'll stand down once they realize we have her. You can fill them in."

"Nicole, tie him up." Jax pushed her forward, causing her to stumble.

Sitting by the headboard, Nicole grabbed the rope out of Nina's hands.

Binding my wrists together, she avoided eye contact with me.

"You're fucking stupid. I could have gotten you out of that shit," I said through a clenched jaw.

"Yeah, gotten me out, and you in? I won't fucking lose you, I've lost too much. You already know that. You won't have to choose between the MC and me, ever again." She tugged on the knotted rope.

"Jesus, Nic, you could have talked to me before taking drastic fucking measures. I'm fucking coming for you." Nicole's head shot up.

"No, you won't. Part of my agreement is to sever all ties with the Condemned Angels. Forget me. Forget whatever we had. It's over. This is the way it's going to be, Jeremy." Jax grabbed Nicole's arm with his good hand and pulled her away. I strained against my restraints.

"Fucking touch her, I swear to God, I'll fucking kill you with my bare hands," I threatened him.

"Pussy," Jax laughed before he hit me over the head with the butt of his gun. Losing consciousness, everything went dark.

CHAPTER 19

CHASE

"CHRIST, ANSWER YOUR FUCKING PHONE!" I YELLED INTO THE RECEIVER. I HAVE BEEN trying to call Jeremy for the last fucking ten minutes because we just spotted Devils running by the clubhouse and what looked like Nicole on the back of a bike.

"He isn't picking up?" Hunter asked. I peered over my shoulder while trying Jeremy's phone again.

"Nah. Let's go over there." We quickly rode over to Jeremy's house, only to find him tied to Nicole's bed knocked the fuck out. What the fuck?

When Jeremy came to, he looked fucking pissed!

"Where the fuck is she?" Jeremy demanded as Hunter and I finished cutting him loose. We all headed down to the kitchen.

"She was spotted with Jax about an hour ago. It didn't look like she was resisting going with them. Care to fucking explain that shit?" I yelled at him, starting to charge him, but Hunter got between us.

"Fuck!" Jeremy ran his hands through his hair and down his face.

"Nic is related to them." Please tell me I just heard him wrong.

"What did you fucking just say? What the fuck does that mean? She's with them? She's Devils? Has Nicole been fucking spying on us?" I know I was jumping to fucking conclusions, but this shit will crush Roxy if she found out.

"Just hold the fuck up for one second! Fucking hear me out. She's not with them, never has and never fucking will be. Nicole is Condemned Angel's property...my fucking property. She went to them in exchange for me." Jeremy was now pacing the room. Hunter and I just stared at him in silence.

"Well, fuck," Hunter mumbled, taking a seat at the kitchen table.

"Now what?" I asked Jeremy. I'd never seen him like this before. Jeremy looked like a madman, fucking pacing and thinking out loud. And now that he just stated that Nicole was his, we gotta go kick some motherfucking ass and get her the fuck back home. I thought we just got done with this shit.

"How many Goddamn times do I have to go see the fucking Devils? Let's get the boys together for an emergency Church meeting. See what Pres says, and go get her," I offered.

The three of us rode to the clubhouse, calling together the brothers for Church. It really hit home seeing Jeremy to the right of Moretti, replacing Charlie. These motherfuckers are going to pay.

"This is fucking déjà vu," I complained as we got started.

"Well, we'd do this ten times over for any of our girls. But this shit ends now. I'm fucking done." Moretti was fucking pissed.

JEREMY

I HAD TO AIR OUT NICOLE'S FAMILY BUSINESS NOW. IT'S FUCKING DO OR DIE. I cleared my throat.

"Is there something you need to say, son?" My father turned his attention to me, the rest of the table did as well.

"Jax...he's Nicole's brother." I couldn't even look them in the eye.

"What?" Moretti boomed.

"She's a Devil?" "She helped them?" "No, fuck you, not our Nicole." Accusations were being thrown around.

"Just hold the fuck on. He's a half- brother, and Nina her half-sister.

98

Nina dropped that shit on her right before they ambushed us."

"So, what the fuck does that mean? She was just waiting to up and leave us?"

"No! Nicole just found out that they are her family. She's been through enough shit in her life. Nicole is innocent and every man sitting at this table knows it. She took my spot, to settle the bad blood we have with the Devils."

"Shit." Dad wiped a hand over his face. I know my Dad thought of Nic as another daughter. She basically grew up in front of him with Roxy. I knew he would never leave her in the hands of the Devils.

"So, what do you want to do about this?" Hunter asked me, his forearms resting on the table. I knew he cared for her too.

"We go in, take them the fuck out, get her and come the fuck home."

"Well, look where that got us the last time," Chase added in. Good fucking point.

"We need to keep this shit out of our town, out of our families, and our club," Moretti stated calmly.

I rubbed the stubble on my face. "Bring in Derrick." I crossed my arms. Derrick the Nomad was ex-military. All those little pills he popped got him kicked out of the service. He was a top performer, a sniper to be exact. He kept that shit on the down-low, and so did we, just in case we needed to call in a favor.

"We take them out from afar, don't get our fucking hands dirty." My Brothers were nodding their heads in agreement.

"Let's vote on it. All in favor of this say 'aye'." Everyone agreed in unison. Thank fuck.

"Well, there you have it, Jeremy."

"Hell fucking right, let's go get my Old Lady." I might as well put that out there now. Everyone stared at me as they paused in mid-standing. "Yeah, you fuckers heard me right. You want to take a vote on it?" I looked them all in the face, and everyone had shit-eating smirks on their faces.

"About fucking time!" Chase slapped my shoulder.

"When do we go?"

"We need to plan this out, let's have Derrick scope the area. It'll take time, son." My father patted my shoulder.

"That's not what I want to fucking hear. Why the fuck can't we go get her now. Jax...I don't trust that motherfucker with Nicole."

"Nicole is a tough girl, she can fend for herself right now. We have a lot at stake here, Jeremy. Think clearly." I stretched my neck, the cracking of my bones filled the room, and I stormed out. I have no fucking patience for this shit. Sticking a cigarette between my lips, I dug in my pocket for my lighter and phone.

Me: Meet me out back in 10

Hunter: Alright

CHAPTER 20

JEREMY

"What brilliant fucking plan do you have now?" Hunter started without even me having to say anything.

"I'm not fucking waiting. We are going to get her tonight. The fuck I know what they have planned for her, and I won't wait. Not another minute. Derrick is on his way- we ride out tonight." I took a long drag of my cigarette.

Hunter rubbed his hand down his face.

"Fuck."

"I know you'd do the same exact shit for her, I don't want to fucking hear it, Hunter." I narrowed my eyes at him.

"Yeah, I know, she's got that voodoo pussy." He wiggled his eyebrows, and I went to charge him, pushing him up against the brick wall.

"You say some fucking shit like that to me ever again, I'll fucking kill you, Hunter." I knew he was just bustin' my balls, but fuck, that shit got under my skin.

"Calm the fuck down. I'm fucking with you. You are right about one thing- I'd do the same. I'm with you, brother." He extended his hand to me. Taking a deep breath, I let out a cloud of smoke and released his now wrinkled shirt. I took his hand and gave it a hard shake.

After Derrick arrived at my house, we suited up. We were all wearing black pants, thermals, cuts, boots, and black bandanas tied around our lower faces. Checking our ammo, we went to mount our bikes and rode out. My Dad was probably going to kill me, but shit, I was VP now, and Nic is my fucking girl. There is no one in this world who can take her away from me. And anyone who gets in my way is a dead man.

The few hours it took to get to Devil's stomping ground were almost more than I could handle. With each and every mile my hatred for Jax grew, along with my wanting for Nicole. That motherfucker was dying tonight.

Nearing their clubhouse, we stopped about a quarter mile back. Parking about five hundred yards out, we left the bikes on an off beaten path. Climbing the dirt path, we found we had a perfect view from up here. Derrick set up his gear; lying down on his stomach he lined his eye up with his scope. Hunter and I lay down on either side of him with binoculars in hand.

They must have been celebrating Jax's homecoming. We could see through the warehouse style windows, the compound was like a night club. There was a large stage with multiple strippers on poles.

"Do you see her?" I pulled down my bandana and wiped the sweat from my forehead.

"No, not yet. I see Jax's bike, so they are in there, somewhere." Derrick stole a quick glance over at me. I didn't like that fucking answer.

There were strobe lights going off, which caught our attention, and a heavy bass rhythm with the rock music. The three of us watched intently, knowing something big was going on.

The stage cleared, and the room went black.

"What the fuck?" Hunter yelled.

"Shut the fuck up. Hold on," I hissed between my teeth. "Someone can fucking hear your loud ass mouth."

"Jer?" Derrick caught both of our attentions. "You'll want to take a look." He nodded to the binoculars I held in my hands. Tightening my grip, I peered through the lenses. There was Nicole, center stage. She wore a black garter belt and stocking set, with a black bra, and sky-high heels. She looked rigid and her fists were clenched at her sides.

Music began, but Nicole stood her ground, holding onto the metal pole in front of her. Men surrounded the base of the stage, yelling for her to dance. Jax appeared from the side of the stage, grabbing Nicole by the crook of her elbow. My jaw tensed. She stumbled a step back in her high heels; he was saying something to her. Nic quickly shut her eyes and nodded her head in understanding. Jax had an evil fucking grin on his face. Slapping her ass before he left her again and the music started up.

"Fuck, is she doing it?" Derrick whispered.

"I don't think she has much of a choice," Hunter answered for me.

Lana Del Rey's "Body Electric" song flooded the speakers. Nicole turned her back to the crowd, tilting her head to the floor, the blue spotlight shown down on her. Slowly getting into the rhythm of the song, she swayed her round hips. Men yelled out for her, catcalls and dollar bills started to get tossed in the air. As the song started, Nicole bent over forward, stretching her garter belt against her ass. I took a deep breath in and licked my lips. Lighting a cigarette, I inhaled, holding onto that breath until my lungs burned.

"Jesus," Derrick mumbled under his breath, but I heard that shit and for a second, I was fucking proud that she was mine.

Facing the pole, Nicole squatted down on her haunches, slowly rolling her pelvis to the pole; her free arm went up under her hair, seductively moving it off her neck. Releasing her hand from her hair, Nicole pushed off her thigh as she rolled her body against the pole as she straightened her back. Slowly Nicole galloped around the pole, she hooked her long legs around it, spinning fast as she locked her thighs, and released her arms and slowly fell backwards.

Nicole's hair splayed out underneath her, her eyes were closed. She didn't want to see them while dancing like this; I could only pray that she was thinking of me. I'm coming, baby, hold the fuck on.

Nicole

Closing my eyelids as I danced for these strangers, took me back to when I was dancing for him. Jeremy, and him alone. While touching my own body, I pictured his hands. All that these men needed was a show. And a show is all they'll fucking get. Jax reminded me of our agreement, and after my dance I was to go to his room, and meet his Old Lady, Eva. What did she want with me? Or what did she and Jax together want with me?

Gripping high on the pole, I lifted my feet up and did a split, slowly sliding down the pole, my pussy was completely flush with the pole, the thin material of my panties was probably now soaked after I've been imagining Jeremy. I crawled on my hands and knees to the end of the stage, which was circle shaped, currently surrounded by big burly men who were tatted up, had half naked women in their laps and beers in their hands. Cash showered down on me as I let my legs spread wide on the stage. My arms splayed out above my head, I rested on my forearms.

I let my hips thrust against the floor to the beat of the music.

JEREMY

Fucking Christ, I need to fuck her when all this is said and fucking done!

Nicole

As the song came to an end, I rolled to my back, letting my hands roam my own body. I tuned out the music. Reaching up, I wrapped my hand around the base of the pole, and pulled myself into a sitting position. I opened my eyes, and everything came back to me. Realization hit me as Jax was walking out to me, helping me off the floor; he guided me offstage and towards his room upstairs. My pulse raced and my heart slammed inside my chest. With every click of my heels up the narrow stairway, I felt my life slipping away from me.

JEREMY

"Where the fuck is she going?"

"The fuck if I know." Hunter let out a frustrated sigh.

"Hold up, the upstairs light just went on," Derrick announced, as he settled in position. Continuing to look for Nicole through the scope of his gun.

"There!" I eagerly licked my lips and adjusted my grip on the binoculars.

The lights flickered in a large open window. Behind the flowing sheer curtains, I could make out Jax's figure entering the room with Nicole behind him. She looked uneasy as he guided her by the small of her back. Gripping the back of her hair, he pulled her head backwards. She grabbed ahold of his hand on her hair, her mouth gaped open in pain.

"Motherfucker, you have a fucking clear shot, Derrick?"

"No, hold the fuck on." He relaxed his shoulders.

Jax suddenly released his grip on Nicole as his attention turned elsewhere in the room. A woman was splayed out on a California king-sized bed. Slowly, she got up, sauntering her way up to Nicole.

"She's in my shot."

"Who?" Hunter and I asked at the same time.

"The redhead."

"Take her out too if you have to, just watch Nicole."

"Don't fucking rush this, Jeremy. Fucking wait till we have a shot," Hunter yelled over to me.

Jax pulled the woman to his side, and they admired Nicole together.

HUNTER

"I HAVE THE SHOT, THE REDHEAD TOO." DERRICK WAITED FOR THE COMMAND FROM Jeremy. I blinked then squinted my eyes to see clearly.

The red hair is what caught my attention. My heart stopped beating in my chest. I was holding my breath as I saw her face turn to the window.

Eva.

"Don't fucking shoot!" I threw my binoculars and scrambled to Derrick. Jeremy quickly grabbed me, trying to pull me off of Derrick.

"What the fuck!" Jeremy shouted.

"You pull that trigger, and I'll fucking kill you, Derrick!" I threatened, scrambling to grab his feet as Jeremy pulled me further away.

"What the fuck is wrong with you?" Jeremy had me in a chokehold.

"The girl. The redhead," I spat out.

"What about her?" Jeremy demanded.

"She's my wife!" Jeremy froze, and then released the hold he had on me. Gasping for air, Jeremy and Derrick stared at me in disbelief.

"DON'T FUCKIN' MOVE!" A voice sounded out over us as barrels of glocks were being shoved in our faces. Fuck, Devils.

ACKNOWLEDGEMENTS

OF COURSE, THE HUBBY COMES FIRST IN THIS. THANK YOU FOR YOUR LOVE AND support through my journey of becoming an indie author. My baby girl, Sofia, for allowing Mama to write! My family and friends, I couldn't be more grateful for such an amazing support team.

Thank you to my Editor, Mandy Smith and her team at Raw Books. Danielle, for all the hot steamy teasers, you've outdone yourself! Lorraine, thank you so much for your time and set of eyes to help proofread Ride Hard! I appreciate all that you do for me, you've helped get the Condemned Angels MC Series off into the book world, and I'm forever grateful! I hope Ride Hard was a big improvement from Burning Desire.

Thank you Brenda Gonet at Gonet Designs for this cover!! You've done a terrific job on the Condemned Angels MC Series, thank you so much!

HUGE thanks to my girl Max Henry at Max Effect Author Services. You are A-M-A-Z-I-N-G! You've brought these books to life with your beautiful formatting! I can't wait to have the third book in your hands so I can see all three of these books together.

Amy Donnelly, thank you so much for the all the awesome graphics, swag designs, steamy countdowns! You rock girl!!

A shout out to all my Beta readers, Mary from Love Between The Sheets, Melinda and Angie from Twinsie Talk, and Tammy from A Slice of Fiction. You ladies are amazing!! I appreciate your help and support with this series.

Last but not least, the readers!! All of your support, feedback and comments from Burning Desire had really impacted me. I loved to hear what everyone thought, and honestly, I was so taken back by the response! I hope you all are pleased with Ride Hard, I hope you're just as eager for Reckless Abandon!

Tell Me What You Think

I appreciate hearing reader opinions about my books.

You can **email** me direct at
heatherleighbooks@gmail.com.

Also, find me on **Goodreads**:
www.goodreads.com/ author/ show/ 8056685.Heather_Leigh

Visit my **Facebook** page at:
www.facebook.com/ HeatherLeighBooks

This book is the second book in a three part series.

AVAILABLE NOW

Condemned Angels # 3

Reckless

Abandon

HEATHER LEIGH

www.ingramcontent.com/pod-product-compliance
Lightning Source LLC
Chambersburg PA
CBHW060940120626
46557CB00003B/1082